Praise for *These Songs I Know By Heart*

"Erin Brubacher's gorgeous new book is a collection of stylish, original, and artfully observed sketches of 21st century romance and modern friendship, and her optimism about the tiny, beautiful connections we make in life is happy-making. *These Songs I Know By Heart* is an odd, winsome, and winning piece of writing."
—Hannah Moscovitch, Governor General's Literary Award–winning author of *Sexual Misconduct of the Middle Classes*

"*These Songs I Know By Heart* is like time spent with a good friend—candid, comforting, and inspiring. Erin Brubacher's spare prose elides the distance between feelings and words, and her sensitive songs are tuned to an artist's pitch."
—Martha Schabas, author of *My Face in the Light*

"One of the quietly radical things about *These Songs I Know By Heart* is the essential goodness of its characters. No forced conflict, no traditional antagonist, no plumbing the fundamental ugliness of its protagonist. What emerges is something more rare and profound: A deeply humane and compassionate compendium of encounter and observation meditating on friendship, motherhood, artmaking, and home."
—Jordan Tannahill, Scotiabank Giller Prize–shortlisted author of *The Listeners*

"A thoughtful, searching novel about connection and love in all its many forms, from fleeting encounters with strangers to bonds with chosen kin. There is a deep generosity in these reflections on art and friendship, uncertainty and loss, and a beautiful openness to the world. This book left me feeling less alone."
—Aimee Wall, Amazon Canada First Novel Award–shortlisted author of *We, Jane*

These Songs I Know By Heart

Erin Brubacher

Book*hug Press
Toronto 2024

Library and Archives Canada Cataloguing in Publication

Title: These songs I know by heart / Erin Brubacher.
Names: Brubacher, Erin, 1979– author.
Identifiers: Canadiana (print) 20230571328 | Canadiana (ebook) 20230571395
  ISBN 9781771669009 (softcover)
  ISBN 9781771668934 (EPUB)
Classification: LCC PS8603.R77 T54 2024 | DDC C813/.6—dc23

The production of this book was made possible through the generous assistance of the Canada Council for the Arts and the Ontario Arts Council. Book*hug Press also acknowledges the support of the Government of Canada through the Canada Book Fund and the Government of Ontario through the Ontario Book Publishing Tax Credit and the Ontario Book Fund.

Book*hug Press acknowledges that the land on which we operate is the traditional territory of many nations, including the Mississaugas of the Credit, the Anishnabeg, the Chippewa, the Haudenosaunee, and the Wendat peoples. We recognize the enduring presence of many diverse First Nations, Inuit, and Métis peoples, and are grateful for the opportunity to meet and work on this territory.

For Phillipa
and Ash

CAMPING WITH ALICE
The Present Perfect

THIS YEAR, WE FOLLOW THE RIVER. THERE'S BEEN SO much rain, we think we might get through. From where we are, the next lake seems close, but I stand up in the boat and see the maze of waterways we'll have to navigate before we're clear. I stand up in the boat because I consider myself invincible in all things I mastered as an adolescent: standing in canoes, improvisational cooking, platonic love, making the best of a bad situation. We follow the current. Alice wants to smoke another cigarette. I should just let her do it: burn through her whole lone pack before we even get there. But I pretend I have some authority and tell her she can't until we clear the reeds. She pretends I have some authority and leaves the cigarette hanging in her mouth, unlit.

Alice and I have been making this trip together since we met, one hot summer a decade ago. This tenth paddle is our anniversary party; it is the quietest party Alice has ever attended. Water lilies and wind. Not that we are silent. The trip is a stream of stories. It is also a sort of personal history lesson. We try to remember each of our birthdays, every piece of work we've ever been paid for, every piece of work we were never paid for, every person we've ever loved, every stranger we've spent more than an hour with, every person we've had sex with, every person we've hurt, every moment we've felt pure joy. We debate the definitions of sex, love, and work. Joy and hurt we agree on.

These lists are interrupted with more and less related revelations:

Alice knows nothing about her grandmother.

I have never read *The Bell Jar.*

Alice knows she could have been a professional swimmer.

I have complicated feelings about Shakespeare.

This last reflection prompts me to tell Alice how, at Shakespeare in the Park—just as Viola was revealing to Orsino and Olivia and everyone that she was a woman—I had somehow managed to go undetected inserting a tampon while sitting in the third row of the audience. It was either that or bleed all over those Canadian Stage High Park cushions. Alice asserts that if I can imperceptibly insert a tampon—while wearing a tight pair of jeans—in the middle of a seated crowd, I can probably do anything.

We stop to acknowledge how lucky we are that it hasn't really rained today. And how lucky we are to be together. We weave through the reeds to the mouth of the river and are on a vast lake, the shape of which seems not to resemble the waterproof map. Alice lights her cigarette and I paddle. She is getting nervous that we won't find a campsite before sunset. I try to distract her with some idle conversation about the watercolours she'll paint tomorrow, or orgasms (generally), or anything I can think of. That reminds her that she forgot to list one of the people she's slept with. He was a meteorologist and his dick was fascinating but too big to work with, so she'd just stare at it and paint it in watercolours. She was in a penis-painting trance for a full week and only got out of bed to change the water. She wants to know if that counts as sex. I've distracted her all right.

We round the point and are quiet for a time as we search the perimeter of the lake. After a while, Alice begins pointing out mushrooms, asking me if she should paint or photograph them tomorrow.

ALICE: I should take a foraging class so we can eat some. But do you think it would be all men in the mushroom-hunting club? Who cares?! What do I care if it's only men in the mushroom club!

I am only half listening, because I'm looking down the water and it has suddenly occurred to me that every man I have ever loved has been afraid of swimming. I bring my keel in and out of the water.

We are having trouble accurately assessing the shape of the lake. I think we are at one point on the map, and Alice is certain we are at another. I reach across our gear and hand her the map. She looks at me.

ALICE: I don't care where we are; we're setting up at that site, right there.

She knows I'll be inclined to paddle around each bend of the lake before making a choice.

ME: Fine.

I steer the boat into the shallow, narrow space between rocks at the nearest site. Alice carefully gets out.

⌂

Alice is a dynamo. She'll be in her prime at eighty. But watching her steady herself getting out of the boat, I know we're both older than we were that summer we met at the backyard party.

In a sense, we were brought together by The Libertine. I had recently moved back to Toronto, and left The Ex-Husband after ten years of shared life. I still loved him, but I thought I might also love The Libertine. Remembering that sensation makes me question if I had any idea what love was at all. I was at the party because I had been invited, and because it was good for me to get out and socialize with new people now that I had completely altered my future. But really I was at the party so I could fraternize with The Libertine. Someone took a photo of me and Alice and The Libertine sitting on a backyard bench, sweat dripping off the three of us in the heat, and he is looking at me and I am pretending not to look back. Alice is entertaining herself as she is capable of doing when she makes up her mind to have a party. In the photo, she is probably thinking about sneaking a cigarette, and delighting herself with this thought. If I saw the image now, I would comment that the vintage tea towel, casually draped around The Libertine's neck, was a clear indicator of empty gestures, but at the time I thought it was impossible to be so attracted to someone with so little character, so I treated him like a blank piece of paper and wrote my hopes on him. But at the backyard party, these hopes were distracted by the energy of Alice. Somehow, Alice and I were alone together in the Dundas West alley adjacent to the backyard, inventing secrets. We found pleasure in the most mundane confessions and dropped our voices whenever the gate opened. The thrill of making a new friend: one entry on the list we compiled called *Pure Joy*.

Alice and I had seen each other around before—we were mutual acquaintances of The Libertine and others—but that day in the alley we knew we had something. She eclipsed the heat, The Libertine, and my uncertainty. She made me feel strong and okay and ready to take better care of myself. I had been having sex off and on with The Libertine for several months, and while it wasn't particularly fulfilling in the moment, and even though I felt consistently terrible afterwards, I was constantly thinking about when and how we would do it again. Someone who has been inside you should never conclude a text with "cheers." Still, I kept sleeping with him. Maybe it was for the usual reasons of loneliness, or perhaps because I was curious about having physical intimacy with somebody so different from The Ex-Husband, who had always been so thoughtful and gentle. Sex with The Libertine was compellingly of the body but also essentially empty, everyone in it for themselves. He seemed hard to quit because I kept seeing him everywhere: buying groceries in Kensington Market, walking through Trinity Bellwoods Park, biking on College Street, on the way to midday meetings across the city, or evening drinks in neighbourhoods I thought were safe. But by the end of the backyard party, I was feeling decisive. I would invite Alice, whom I barely knew, to go on a canoe trip, and I would delete The Libertine's phone number. Miraculously, from that moment on, I never saw The Libertine again and, more miraculously, Alice agreed to go camping.

⌂

I am starting the fire while Alice lays out the tent and unwinds the tarp rope. Everything is a little damp and it's going to be difficult. Alice feeds my ego by telling the story of how I once kept the fire going through three full days of cold rain. I hunch over, fanning the flames in the kindling with a metal plate. Alice sticks her head out from our precariously erected tent.

ALICE: Nice work! The only problem is you're wearing too many clothes and I can't get a good enough view of that great ass!—Careful of your back, mate! Bend your knees!

She asks me how we're going to maintain and improve our bodies, purely for the purpose of ease on the trip as we age. We want to be old ladies starting the fire and setting up the tent. We don't want to miss a year of this.

⛺

Alice owns a stationery shop in Toronto called I Really Need You. The main attraction is her watercolour cards. The most popular one is an ice cream cone with two scoops on it, that looks like testicles when turned upside down. The second most popular is her Wonderland mushrooms thank-you card series. While I join Alice in the two-person parts of the tent set-up, we talk about a new card collection she is developing on thoughtfulness. She says the most thoughtful thing she can think of is the simple act of bringing a friend flowers for no reason. The first thoughtful thing that comes to my mind is Q-tips.

After four years apart, I spent one week with The Ex-Husband, in a friend's vacant house, in a small French village. I was between homes and took up a self-made residency there, where it wasn't so far for him to visit me. I picked flowers and put them in water. I filled a bowl with fruit. We compared souvenirs. The first morning, I asked him if he had any Q-tips. He didn't. Near the end of the week, he washed and hung our clothes the way he used to, and we sat in the kitchen, pouring afternoon glasses while they dried. He took our clothes off the line and folded them, as we had folded time. It was an overdue goodbye we hadn't been ready for sooner. On the last morning, we walked to the general store to get him some food for his journey home. I waited outside. We went back to the house to collect his bags and make our final farewells. I walked him to the bus stop, and when I returned, there were Q-tips in the bathroom. The gesture was so perfectly him.

I wonder if he wouldn't want me sharing these stories. He might find this whole thing self-indulgent. But if you are reading this now, it means he said I should go ahead and write what I like. Or he asked me to alter things, and I already have.

⛺

The larger branches have caught flame and Alice has the tent under control.

ALICE: What do you think of orchids?

ME: Orchids are beautiful. But I don't really care for them. They're too perfect and fragile. I prefer wildflowers.

ALICE: Oh yeah. Wildflowers are the go, mate.

I add a log to the fire and watch it burn.

ME: Hey—what's an appropriate thank-you card to send to your ex-mother-in-law for no particular reason?

The Ex-Husband's mother still writes me once a year, at Christmas or New Year's. She doesn't say much, her sentiments usually expressed through an e-card with exploding fireworks or a series of emoticons she learned how to use at the public library. It is very kind.

ALICE: I'll paint you a lily pad right now. Before the light goes!

Alice takes out her watercolours and I take out my pocket knife, a gift from The Turtle, to open the vac pack of sausages before laying them on the grill. I slice a bulb of fennel in half and arrange the pieces between the sausages. Alice paints till dark. She carefully hangs her lily-pad paintings from the tent fly rope with clothes pegs, then joins me on the log bench. I tend the fire and lay the loaded grill on top of it. We place our ready plates on a tree-trunk table, no doubt fashioned by a group of industrious men confusing nature for a project, and watch the fat drip out of the casing. We pass a flask of whisky back and forth, listening to the circle of trees around us sway, from time to time.

There are no people around to worry about. The water is calm as the wind comes and goes. The moon is massive.

My dad says he always likes to get my emails. Even if they just say:

Hi dad,
I'm looking at the moon.
xo

The moon is bright enough to wash our plates by. I think about writing my dad a letter, and finish washing up before going to get some paper from my notebook, in the fun bag inside the tent. But once I'm in there, I don't want to get out. I call Alice in.

In the tent, we read stories aloud. Words float from our mouths in the shared air. This year, our short story author is Kathleen Collins. Her writing is amazing and Alice wants superlatives.

ALICE: Miranda July is a lazy ass for blurbing Kathleen's book with just "sexy, radical and intimate."

She pauses to study the rest of the book jacket.

ALICE: Come on! That's all you got, Miranda?! Kathleen is absolutely fabulous and deserves more words!

Then Alice gets into her name theories—which I love. She used to leave me a voice mail a week, describing the nature and character of a person named Magnus, or Mel, or Carol...

ALICE: At least she's a Kathleen and not a Kathy. A Kathy is a Katherine who deserves better than her name. A Katherine knows what she's worth and doesn't forget it. A Kathleen... Hmmmm, I'll have to think about that one... I do prefer a Catherine with a *C* to a *K*, but a Kathleen has got to be a *K*, so I won't hold that against her.

Alice enjoys inventing things to make a fuss about. She turns the page, blinding me with her headlamp before starting the next story. Midway through, she changes her mind.

ALICE: "Sexy, radical and intimate" is actually pretty good. Miranda always knows what she's doing.

We fall asleep.

One year, before I knew Alice, I lived on an island. On that island, I met three women: one with red hair, one with great legs, and one with talking eyes. Knowing each of them gave me a rush.

THREE WOMEN

I
The Redhead and I met once a week at a scene-study class at the local theatre, and she would drive me home afterwards. She'd park outside my place and we'd sit in the car and talk for an hour each night before I got out. One night, she turned to me and said, You're going to leave, aren't you? In that moment I felt all the space she held for me shrink. She knew I would not stay on the island, and I watched the armour fold around her heart. Have a good night, she said, with kindness but without warmth. That moment would go on a list of heartbreaks.

II
I met Great Legs at a local brewery. She would have a drink when she finished work, and I would have a drink

while I wrote in my notebook at a table, by the window. I knew she had great legs because we spent a great deal of our time together browsing and trying things on in the thrift store at the end of the street where we both happened to live. A few days before I moved away, I tried to make a big deal out of it. I talked about when we might see each other again and promised correspondence. She was direct and clear with me. This is it; we had our time, she said.

III
I knew Talking Eyes from the community darkroom. We would go for long walks out of town, on the stony beaches, and make pictures of each other with fucked-up film that she'd had in the trunk of her car for a year after buying it, already expired. She was a person who made you consider things. You could leave a question blowing on the bay and she'd catch it with a look. I don't remember how that time ended, but many years later, after she'd moved back home to another sea town, I wrote her a Facebook message saying I'd be in her local airport for a two-hour layover. I asked if she would meet me there. We sat in the small airport bar, holding hands and drinking shitty beer while recounting the evolution of our lives.

If Alice or I moved away tomorrow, I believe our future would be some version of my meeting with Talking Eyes in the airport. That said, I owe my friendship with Alice, in part, to staying in one place.

I am thinking about The Redhead, Great Legs, and Talking Eyes when I wake up in the tent. I don't tell Alice about them because she is prone to inventing jealousies for something to make a fuss about, and I am feeling too sentimental to joke about beloved ghosts.

Alice is the present and ongoing manifestation of unpredictable friendship. She is not a person with whom I grew up, or someone I will ever work with—in a life that is populated by other artists and projects that are constantly blurring the lines of personal and professional intimacy. We don't have a community of people who keep us connected and, if either of us stopped making an effort, we could very easily fade into each other's hindsight. We could disappear into the city and conceivably never cross paths. She could become a person from another island of my past.

⌂

I met The Ex-Husband the autumn that I was twenty. It was a hike organized by the University of Bordeaux, where I was studying on exchange. I was ten days off the plane and could barely speak French. I remember gesticulating wildly to the whole group to indicate that I didn't know what our guide was talking about. The Ex-Husband is the one who answered me. He couldn't speak much English, but he gesticulated back, miming out the animals and geological features the guide was referencing. We spent the rest of the day each trying to learn something about the other, in a string of single words and with the use of very few sentences. We were both bilingual by the end of the year.

At the end of summer, I returned to Canada—and then flew back to France the next spring. When I'd been back in France for about a month, couch-surfing with friends and semi-living in The Ex-Husband's student housing, I went to an Internet café and wrote My Childhood Friend an email:

Subject: am I ridiculous?
Last night he announces that the idea of living with another person—me specifically—is "plus pensable" now than when we first met, but that he doesn't really see himself living with anyone or having children. I'm not saying that I plan on having children any time soon, but... Is it ridiculous that this seems problematic to me, when I'm only at the barely adult age of 22?? Should I just calm the fuck down and stop taking everything so seriously?

My Childhood Friend responded:

Subject: No, you're not.
For one thing. I know that having children is really important to you. You interact with kids the way you make art. It's so clearly something you are passionate about, and something you have a knack for. And I heartily believe that through raising children someday (as well as through doing all the other things you will do), you will make an irreplaceable contribution to the well-being of our world. I can TOTALLY understand that what he said would seem like a bit of a wall. I mean, it's one thing if a person says that when he's sixteen (I said that myself when I was sixteen—and seventeen, and eighteen, and nineteen...). But once someone is well into his twenties, I think it's fair to say that his ideas about the way he wants to live his life are settling down a bit. Not to say that minds don't keep changing—throughout life. But still. I can see why you are given pause. Not only that, I think it IS a bit of a wall for

him to say "I can't see myself living with anyone" when
you have gone back to France to be with him. What the hell
was he expecting?

After that, The Ex-Husband and I hitchhiked across Ireland. It was a wonderful trip that I thought would be our last. Back in Bordeaux, after brushing our teeth in the tiny sink of his residence room, I told him I was ready to let go.

We can end this now, I said. I know you love me and I know you don't want what I want. I understand.

Non, he said. C'est bon, ça va. I will have an enfant with you.

And then things went on for a decade. We lived together, in a different city every year, and somehow I think that moving kept us together—being an island of two. We got married and became citizens of each other's countries. We were each other's teachers, from foreign lands of personality. We shaped each other's values. We made each other better thinkers and learned to love our bodies through the other's gaze. We took people in and cared for them and were ourselves taken in and cared for. Together we were parents and children to other travellers.

After our meeting in her local airport, Talking Eyes decided to come to Toronto for a visit. I lived alone, in an old four-storey apartment building, on a short cul-de-sac between neighbourhoods: to the east, St. James Town—one of Canada's most densely populated high-rise communities; to the north, Rosedale—one of Toronto's wealthiest pockets of single-family dwellings; and to the west, the Village. Talking Eyes thought walking through these neighbourhoods was like travelling to different countries, and it was. It was easy to feel distant from one while in another, even if one could walk through all three in under a half hour.

On the Sunday morning of her stay, Talking Eyes announced that she wanted to go to Mass. Her Catholicism had always surprised me: for her it was all about love. (She drew hearts on everything.) My cul-de-sac connected to another short cul-de-sac, and at the end of that joining street was Our Lady of Lourdes, with its beautiful dome basilica. It seemed only right to know what was happening in a public gathering place, at the end of my very own street, so I said I would go. There were at least 450 people at the eleven-thirty Mass—one of *six* Sunday Masses and *twenty-four* weekly masses that I had been completely unaware of.

◁△

My maternal grandmother was Catholic. I was never quite sure of the nature of her faith: it felt to me more like a social norm, or an insurance policy, than a question of spirituality. But, in any case, just in case, when I was a baby my grandmother snuck me out of the house and baptized me. So when Alice asked me to be the godmother for her daughter Marigold, we supposed that I was technically Catholic. Alice assured me that the baptism of Marigold was, for her, more a matter of tradition than religion, but still I clarified that I would not utter any god language to which I did not subscribe. Alice said that was fine.

There were several children being baptized on Marigold's day, and we waited our turn for the rites and rituals, in a way that felt like a cross between a sacred ceremony and an appointment to renew your driver's licence at Service Ontario. When it came time for me to repeat the priest's words, I whispered a promise of my own phrasing. I promised to always be there for Marigold, to look out for her and hold her close. Then, when I was supposed to use the holy water to draw a cross on her forehead, instead I drew a small heart.

⌂

ALICE: What about a coffee?

This is Alice's way of telling me to get out of the tent and make her a coffee. We've been lazing side by side, in our fabric cocoons, drifting in and out of sleep and conversation for over an hour. We've been listening to the breeze.

While we drink our coffee, I read to Alice by the lake. In addition to the short stories by Kathleen Collins, this trip we brought a book about the artist Sophie Calle. I read Alice the introduction. For her 1979 piece *The Sleepers*, Calle invited people to take turns sleeping in her bed. She asked people to give her eight hours of their sleep and to allow themselves to be seen and photographed by her, in slumber. The idea of accepting an offer from a stranger strikes me now, more than ever, as a supreme act of generosity.

I've always taken the general concept of kindness + strangers very much to heart. This has been illustrated by countless unremarkable events. Like the time I stepped on a piece of glass.

I stepped on some glass in my kitchen and got a wart on the ball of my foot. Or I stepped on the glass, broke the skin, then went to the YMCA and got a wart from the change room, or the steam room, or just walking around that great place in general. Or maybe I stepped on the piece of glass and then got a wart from the shower of The Illustrator I met on Tinder, whose apartment I stayed over at, that same week I stepped on that glass. In any case, a few days after I pulled the glass from my foot, a wart developed in the exact same spot. So at least the cause of vulnerability was clear.

I love the YMCA, especially the YMCA change room, with the steam room and hot tub. I love being amongst all the women, of all ages and shapes. I love hearing them talk to each other, the strangers and the friends. I love that no one is on their phones and most people are comfortable enough to be naked in a situation in which it makes sense to be naked. I loved that my friend The Weaver and I regularly made plans to meet at the Y to exercise, and instead spent hours there, vaguely working out, before moving to the hot tub to exchange counsel about the challenges of collaboration, the projects we were managing, the kids we were mentoring, and ways to find a better "work-life balance." For these reasons, I've decided to absolve the Y, and just say that The Illustrator gave me the wart. Better than an STI, I guess. Plus I knew The Illustrator and I were done anyway, after he pontificated that a person could be either a good artist or a good parent—not both.

(I read somewhere about two mid-career writers in a bar at a literary festival. The first was pregnant and the second, gesturing to the first writer's belly, said: You must be worried about falling behind. She paused before responding that he must be worried about a lack of human experience.)

I searched "wart treatments" and there were literally hundreds. My favourite was a literary folk remedy: *Rub a dusty, dry toad on warts, and they will disappear.* I went to see a chiropodist at the Artists' Health Network, who told me that the best way to treat the wart was for her to freeze my foot and poke me with a needle, one hundred times.

When I do this, she said, the virus will be introduced to your body for your immune system to fight. Biology—cool, right? That's how the body works: first it needs to develop an awareness.

That's how the spirit works too, I thought.

After the chiropodist froze my foot and poked me with one hundred needles, I tried to stand up and immediately collapsed. I was a few blocks from my favourite coffee shop in Kensington Market, so I limped through the hospital and out to the street, where I considered my options. A car slowed at a stop sign and I found myself gesturing slightly to the person in the passenger seat. She rolled down the window and I heard myself say, Um, hi. Sorry. My foot is completely frozen and I can't walk on it. I just need to get to the end of the street—would I be able to ride with you? I figured I was standing right next to the hospital, so I would seem legit. She and the driver looked at each other, and then one of them said they had too much stuff in the back, and the other sort of shrugged regret before they drove off. It wasn't a big deal, but it made me cry. I'd been counting on a little kindness.

△

About the *Sleepers* project, Sophie Calle said she thought that people said "yes" when asked a question to which they had not already learned to answer "no."

ALICE: I would have slept in Sophie's bed if she asked me.

ME: I know you would have. You slept in a tent with me after three beers in an alley.

△

I've found what Sophie said to be true. When The Ex-Husband and I lived in Amsterdam, I was nearing the conclusion of a years-long, city-spanning project on public life. I'd made a list of colours to follow: red, yellow, green, blue, black, white. I'd start each day at the entrance to the courtyard of the building where we lived, and wait for the first person I saw cycling, in any direction, and wearing red—the first colour on my list. I'd follow them. When that person stopped, I stopped too, and gently approached them: I have an invitation for you, I'd say, handing them a note in a tiny envelope. They hadn't learned to say no to a small sweet envelope in a safe public space. Sometimes they would open it in front of me, and other times slip it into a pocket, before slipping away themselves.

From each geographic point where I gave an invitation, I'd

wait for the first cyclist I saw wearing the next colour on my list. So, beginning from my own place of residence, I followed a "neighbour" who led me somewhere, and then followed the next neighbour based on where the previous one had led me. Each invited person determined the subsequent invitation, and took me to places unknown.

The invitation read:

Beste buur,
Hierbij nodig ik je uit, om mij uit te nodigen, om je te verge-
zellen tijdens een van je dagelijkse openbare bezigheden. Ik
ben geïnteresseerd naar het openbare leven in Amsterdam.
Wellicht kunnen we samen er iets over uitvinden terwijl
we wat tijd met elkaar door brengen, als stadsgenoten, als
onbekenden die een stad delen.

Dear Neighbour,
I would like to invite you, to invite me, to join you, in an
act of your everyday public life. I am interested in finding
out what public life is made of. I'm hoping we can learn
something about it, while spending a bit of time together,
as strangers who share a city.

I was invited to do lots of everyday Amsterdam things, including: drink morning coffee in a square, feed ducks, dig in a community garden, walk to a meeting from one office building to another, wait for a child after school, window-browse sex providers, attend a party at a museum, collect garbage, and make and sell stroopwafels in a local market.

The whole public-life project had started, unintentionally, the year before, in Paris. After four years of living in Canada, The Ex-Husband had wanted to move back to France and, coincidentally, I was offered a job in Paris teaching visual art and theatre at an international lycée. Paris was the last place in France The Ex-Husband had wanted to go, but he was also practical, so we tried to find a sense of home there. It was hard to find the city promising, with a husband who hated the people, the traffic, the dirt, and especially the noise, with no friends or collaborators, and with no place to live. I remember us sleeping on the floor of a relative's studio apartment, me slipping out in the mornings to work at a new and exhausting job, and then lining up for hours to look at apartments, holding the standard French dossier containing a pay stub and other documents that would determine our tenant pecking order. I wanted to feel settled and grounded in this place. I wanted to sleep in a bed. I wanted to make a home that we could host in, if we ever met anyone to host.

We finally found an apartment above what looked like a quiet old man's pub in the 14ème. We dragged our bags up two narrow flights of stairs, and I began unpacking immediately. Less than an hour later, vibrations began from below—blaring Gypsy Kings' "Bamboléo," followed by Celine Dion's "Where Does My Heart Beat Now."

Non non non non, said The Ex-Husband. As Celine started singing, he began repacking our bags. I just looked at him. I didn't want to go anywhere.

It's not so bad. Maybe it's just on Thursdays? I offered.

Maybe optimism would have been futile in that moment, but that's what I wanted.

Weeks later, we found a tiny apartment in the 15ème arrondissement. Once we were somewhat settled, The Ex-Husband spent his free time foraging in man-made forests on the outskirts of Paris. He was looking for solitude and I needed contact. I walked out into the city, with my camera and no clear objective, and waited to see what came back to me.

Soon, every Saturday, I would go to Parc Georges Brassens, to photograph people reading in public. I'd notice these readers in public space and ask if I could make portraits of them, just as and where they were. I didn't try to convince anyone, and a number of people did say no. I would start to ask my question and they'd already be waving me off—until they registered the twin-lens Rolleiflex hanging around my neck.

Vous-pouvez regardez, si vous voulez, I'd say, inviting them to have a closer look. They'd watch me pop open the hood of my camera and peer down through its ground glass, and I'd watch as the Rollei changed their minds.

Bon, d'accord, they'd say. They would continue reading, and I would make the picture.

One person specified that she didn't want her picture *on the Internet*, but if I was using *that* camera, it was okay. I told her that I might scan the negative and it might, in fact, end up *on the Internet*. Her feeling was, though, that it was okay if it was for *art*. My Rolleiflex seemed to be some kind of art guarantor. (The Ex-Husband had said he would feel the same way—to this day, he has never owned a smart phone or joined a single social media platform.)

After each portrait, its subject and I would have a conversation. I would ask about what they were reading, taking note of the title along with other quickly scribbled details:

19 secondes 83 centièmes
Man with one hand in his pocket

Les hommes qui n'aimaient pas les femmes
He can't get into the book

L'Œuvre de Dieu, la part du Diable
Nose picker

Les bienfaits du régime crétois
Skeptical

La rage d'être libre
With daughter in Rollerblades

La métamorphose
Memorizing text for theatre class

Je ne suis pas enceinte: Enquéte sur le déni de grossesse
Photo okay, but wants no contact after

Une relation dangereuse
Make sure to get his "good side"

La campagne présidentielle n'a pas eu lieu
Alone in a circle of empty chairs

La fin des princes
Said yes because her granddaughter would want her to

Ubu roi
That man who said no a few months ago—

—I remember that man. I remember him watching me photograph other people. Maybe he'd been watching me for weeks, considering the invitation. I recognized him immediately, and felt the memory of his earlier rejection make my face hot when we caught eyes. After a while I looked right at him, and he motioned for me to come over and take his picture.

Bon, on y va, he said.

Sometimes I'd talk with people for a long time after making the picture. Hours. Their stories made my own more meaningful, and less important. We were all just parts of the city.

We talked about public life and how it described the nature of a city and culture. We talked about photography and *le droit à l'image* vs. *le droit de l'image*. *Le droit* à *l'image* is a legal term that refers to the right an individual has to the use of their own image—an image in which they figure. *Le droit* de *l'image* is a spin on the former, referring to the right of the image itself, as a part of our collective history. For example, is a photo I could make right now—of Alice drinking her coffee in an enamel mug, on a rock in Algonquin Park—a photo *of Alice*? Or is it a photo of a forty-something woman, in the late summer of this time and place in history?

One reader's book was called *Les cent plus beaux poèmes de la langue française*. It had a dark red velvet cover. As I was motioning to leave, the reader handed me her book.

Prendre-le, she said.

It is not the sort of gift I can imagine myself parting with, and yet I know it never returned with me to Canada. I wonder if there is someone, somewhere, reading it now.

⌂

It's raining now. We pause our reading, and I run for Alice's lily-pad paintings, still hanging exposed from the tent rope. Alice secures the tarp that we only half installed last night. When we're camping, I don't mind the rain. It's better if it doesn't rain while we're paddling in, but once we've made a dry space to sit and read, write, play cards, drink coffee, and stare at the water, I don't mind.

In Toronto, the weather makes me sad. This is a relatively new thing. As I approached forty, several irritating things happened: I suddenly understood seasonal affective disorder, I stopped being able to sleep through anything, and people started talking to me about freezing my eggs. Apparently, when a woman is twenty-five, the likelihood of her getting pregnant is 25 per cent every month if not using contraception. So statistically, my doctor explained to me, when you're twenty-five and trying, chances are you'll be pregnant within four months. By the time you're thirty-eight, that likelihood has dropped to 12 per cent. And then at thirty-nine you're suddenly down to 7 per cent—it goes downhill fast from there. And of course, while this fertility percentage decreases, the percentage of people talking to you about freezing your eggs climbs. These people could be your parents, or practical strangers.

Alice got pregnant at forty, without even trying.

⌂

When I was twenty-four, The Ex-Husband and I were married in a little house on an Arctic beach of Kangiqsualuk ilua in Nunavut. Only four other people were present: our justice of the peace (a new friend who was born into the warm weather of Jamaica and had chosen a life in the Arctic), the couple who offered their home for the ceremony (an Inuk politician from Iqaluit and a distant relative from Toronto), and a lawyer from Saskatchewan. It was an official kind of marriage, for both love and for papers, with a spoken clause: no longer than it lasts. The Ex-Husband, an anti-materialist, was never a believer in symbols. Still, a few days before our wedding, I spontaneously bought us rings carved of caribou antler. My new husband reluctantly wore his for a week and I eventually took mine off too.

For my twenty-fifth birthday, my mum mailed me my grandmother's wedding ring, via regular post—talk about a leap of faith. I wore it because I loved my grandmother, but also because of that searching for something I could wear in some relationship to my relationship with The Ex-Husband. Of course, the ring felt more like a symbol of marriage to my matriarchal line than it did to my husband. In hindsight, I see I was looking to imbue an object with the power to make me feel more solid in my marriage. Some talisman to hold us together in the world outside of our own private island: to make us last longer. I wanted to feel the intention of forever, whether we believed in it or not.

We were still using two kinds of birth control.

⛺

My Childhood Friend has a child called The Fig. Before The Fig was born, My Childhood Friend and I, both secular symbol makers and not godparent-inclined, decided I would be The Fig's "mentor." I was there the day she was born, and the moment I met her was one of four times that I have cried for happiness. Every year for The Fig's birthday we make a cake together. For her third birthday, the cake was strawberry with cream-cheese icing, fresh berries, and a dozen kinds of artificial edible decorations in unnatural colours. I'd laid all the ingredients out on my kitchen table and constructed a tower from them, balancing tubes and canisters on top of bags of flour and bowls of berries. I was quite pleased. The Fig would like it. Then My Childhood Friend called to say The Fig was having a tantrum and didn't want to put on any warm clothes to leave the house, and could I come over to their place instead?

A three-year-old cannot actually stand you up. A three-year-old is just being a three-year-old. Still, it made me sad to take the tower down. After I'd packed up all the ingredients to take to their house, My Childhood Friend called again to say The Fig had her coat on and wanted to come to my place. That's how it goes sometimes. Which is why it's always best to have flexible expectations. Especially around birthdays.

The idea that Alice and I should try to remember each of our birthdays came on our second trip, when Alice was complaining about a three-kilometre portage. As a distraction, I asked her to tell me about her most recent birthday and then go backwards, year by year, as far as she could remember. It took the whole three kilometres and some of the next lake to finish the exercise. It was such a beautiful thing to listen to. I promised Alice that, over the course of the coming year, from the day I turned thirty-three until the day I'd turn thirty-four, I would ask thirty-three people to tell me about their birthdays, starting from how old they were then and counting back as far as they could remember. My favourite parts were the pauses—watching people speechlessly search their memories.

Making promises to Alice is how I follow through with lots of ideas. Somehow, telling Alice I'll do something makes doing it necessary. Right now I'm working on a series of poems called *Popular Songs*. I told Alice I would write one for every question and every certainty I've felt about love for another person. I wonder how I'll know when I'm finished.

Under the tarp, Alice is tapping on a rock with her watercolour brushes as if she were playing a drum kit. I tell her the story of nineteen-year-old me and My First Real Romance, and how we once spent an afternoon without words, making instruments of every implement in his kitchen. He opened and closed lids, I let the faucet drip, and we made percussion from each bowl and bucket. After a full hour of the kitchen orchestra, I pulled the cutlery drawer right out and dumped the whole thing on the floor in one swift, clattering move. My First Real Romance broke the subsequent silence, by belting out the overture from *Anything Goes*.

We left the contents of the drawer strewn across the floor with a note for his housemates that read, *imagine what happened here*, written with a marker we'd found in the drawer. Before we fled the scene, I took the cap back off the marker, took hold of My First Real Romance's arm, and wrote in cursive letters along the line of his most pronounced vein: *I Get a Kick Out of You*. (I have never found it best to leave feelings unexpressed.)

Things went on like this for most of a school year. There was so much joy in that house. I was in love with My First Real Romance, but I loved the home more. The family we made of the house's roommates and their companions. The elaborate dinners of early-adult cooks, the single desktop computer we acquired—that ten of us shared, taking shifts at all hours of the night to type up term papers in a variety of liberal arts subjects. It all ended quite dramatically, during a 6:00 a.m. rehearsal for the outdoor promenade production of *Twelfth Night* My First Real Romance and I had been making together. It felt like the whole university town woke to the sound of my chest cracking.

ALICE: That's probably why you almost bled all over those Shakespeare in the Park cushions; you were probably having some traumatic body memory.

ME: I think that's a little over the top.

ALICE: Heartbreak *is* over the top.

◭

Love comes, and goes.

I made a choice when I was thirty-one. My choice was this: leave The Ex-Husband or have a baby with him. We'd just moved back to Toronto together, to finally give it a go. I don't know why I left it so long. Maybe I didn't believe we were getting any older. Maybe all our travelling kept us in one place. Maybe I always knew he would be doing it for me, and I didn't want it that way. I'd always be more professionally driven, I'd always be able to make more money, we wouldn't succeed at switching off, he'd end up doing all the child care, and we'd both resent each other.

I remember sobbing into my mother's pillow. She asked me a very simple question: Would you feel so badly if you didn't think you were hurting him?

No.

The days before he flew home to France were long. In our last week together, we got up before sunrise and searched for places in the city where no one would know us, where we didn't have to speak. There's nothing to say when there's no future.

◭

ALICE: Hey, mate! How's this for a title for a tattoo parlour? It Hurts Less Than a Broken Heart—it's good, right?!

ME: It is. Okay, I think I'm done my poem about The Painter.

Whitney Houston

One night, we watch boats. Another night, ducks.
We debate the appeal of nature and find a compromise:
rolling hills of plastic grass.
A place to hold each other a little.

We close our eyes an listen, to the cover band
across the turf — when we look up, we're surrounded
by a circle of teenagers, staring.
(Tomorrow, the poetic one will write that
"old people still make-out in public,"
in her in-class essay on perspectives.)

Drunk and fearless, they serenade us
as the cover band accompanies: oh, ~~I wanna dance~~
~~They wanna feel that heat with Somebody too.~~
Dancing circles around us, ~~said band~~

~~They scream and laugh and prophecize~~
they prophesize our future.

They tell us we'll remember them forever,
and we do.

41

When I was thirty-five, I took a train to visit The Painter.

The Painter wanted nothing to do with children. He offered this information in bed one night, with characteristic tenderness. I lay there in silence, wondering if I should get up and leave. What was I doing there? While The Painter was never someone with whom I had considered children as a possible outcome, I somehow found his statement shocking. I had been fantasizing about having a child alone. So I lay there, still holding his hand, thinking: If I was a mother, could I be here like this with someone who despised my child for being a child? I decided to see how I felt in the morning. We came again and went to sleep.

That night, lying next to The Painter, I dreamt of Alice at seventeen. She was inconsolable. When I asked her what was the matter, she said she was just grieving the end of her childhood. I woke thinking that The Painter was still grieving the fact that he'd had to endure a childhood at all. I put my hands on his face and held him until it was time to go.

Love comes, goes, and then comes back again.

I fell in love with The Turtle on a New Year's Day. Early in that new year, he wrote me a compliment: your voice is warm with a hint of always laughing. It made me feel seen. It was the feeling of finding a person inside the song you have always sung but never known.

⛺

The rain is warm. Alice writes postcards under the tarp while I walk barefoot on a patch of sphagnum—bright green peat moss. I think about the desire to walk on things, to plant one's own feet on cushioned moss, or a series of uneven rocks. To have felt a place beneath you. Maybe it's about leaving an invisible trace of yourself too. Like when The Turtle and I were in Kyoto, and I took my shoes off to walk on a small wooden bridge near Ryōan-ji. I thought if I could feel the curve of that bridge on the balls of my feet, I would somehow leave a mark of myself there.

I wonder what happens after a heavy rain on Ryōan-ji's Zen temple garden, where the gravel rocks are raked, in the same formation, year after year. What needs to be reset and reordered? What traces are left by time and weather, after five hundred years of tending and preserving patterns?

⟁

I call The Turtle *Turtle* because that is his name, and because that's how he introduced himself. Everyone else calls him Shell. He has never said, "Call me Shell," to me or to anyone else. Still, Shell is what he has always been called. At first, when I called him Turtle, I felt people notice. I didn't particularly enjoy noticing them notice, but I'll admit that my calling him Turtle was an act of intention. Shell was one half of a couple for twenty years before we met, and I guess, for me, Shell was a person I didn't know—a person only written into sentences with another person's name next to his. So I called him by his name, as a small way of making a place for me and The Turtle in a sentence.

⟁

ME: See that?

I call out to Alice, pointing to an unofficial path leading away from the site, past the patch of sphagnum and into the woods, somewhere.

ME: That's a desire line.

Alice looks up from under the tarp.

ALICE: Tell me.

ME: Desire lines are unplanned trails made by repeated footfall. They usually represent the most easily navigated route between an origin and destination. They're shortcuts. Should we see where it goes?

I like the idea of paths made where there are none, because of a common need. This trip is a common need.

ALICE: Should we go nude?

Alice is already taking her dry clothes off under the tarp. I'm only wearing a button-up shirt, and it's already soaked.

ME: Sure.

Alice loves the idea of "going nude." I pull my shirt off over my head and we trudge off, further wearing the trail. I like how desire lines don't take up any more space than they require. They are simple functional carvings that respond to use. If they are no longer needed, nature will take care of it. The trail leads to a rock point. It looks deep enough to dive.

ALICE: I'll climb down and check it out.

Alice carefully makes her way down a series of smaller rocks and, when she gets to the water, looks up at me.

ALICE: I wish I had a camera right now! Seriously, your body has never looked better. And that hair, man. It's wild! I love it.

Alice says these things every year, and she always means it. It's a thing I can count on.

⛺

The Weaver is reliably in touch. If she doesn't hear from me, I hear from her. She once told me that I decided to be her friend and made it happen. That does sound like me. But the ongoing commitment is totally reciprocal.

⛺

The weekend Talking Eyes came to visit, after we got back from Mass at Our Lady of Lourdes, I asked her about bangs. When we first met, Talking Eyes was a hairdresser. She said she became a hairdresser to have a tangible impact on people's lives. She had since gone back to school and become a teacher for the same reason—she is committed to this pursuit in whatever she does. Her small acts are reliably transformative.

When I asked her about bangs, Talking Eyes looked at me briefly, raised her scissors, and, in two swift moves, cut off fifteen inches of hair at the front of my head.

We're doing it, she said—which at that point seemed clear. When you asked me to give ya bangs ten years ago, I told ya it was a big commitment. But now we've lived enough to know it's pretty small on the commitment scale, right? It'll grow back, she said as she continued to cut.

The bangs were not an unequivocal success. Lots of friends said things like, *Oh they're fine*. But I liked them. There was something very freeing about the simple fact of having a clear, unobstructed view.

What matters is that you're changing it up, said The Boy. You're still trying new things.

I have known The Boy since he was twelve. He is now in his twenties, but he will always be The Boy to me. He is a great dancer and asks really good questions. He sometimes calls for advice about cooking, and about love. The Boy lives near Alice's shop. He and Alice both like paper, notebooks, old stamps, and dressing up. I like that they've come to know each other. Though, one time, their acquaintance got me in trouble. It got me in trouble with the white pantsuit.

There was a street festival in Alice's neighbourhood, and everyone was dressing up. I was in Alice's shop that afternoon and decided to stick around. Alice said she could loan me something to wear. As Alice thumbed through her closet, she lingered at a sleeveless, strapless, one-piece, tuxedo-style white pantsuit. It had wide legs, a fitted bust, and fabulous buttons down the back.

I mistook her lingering for a proposal and said, Oh yeah.

What about that?

I suspect that if I could rewind that moment and watch Alice's body language and facial expressions as I tried on the white pantsuit, I would have known for certain that wearing it was not a good idea. But in the moment, I was delighting in the white pantsuit and thinking it looked good on me. Really good. Alice did let me wear it to the street festival. She even took a photo of me, in the middle of the street modelling it, holding a bunch of helium balloons, and later put that photo in her shop window display. But at the end of the evening, when I left the neighbourhood festival still wearing the white pantsuit, Alice was not happy. She did not want the white pantsuit out of her sight.

A few weeks later, The Boy was in Alice's shop and saw the photo of me in the window. Oh, that's the ensemble she was wearing when I saw her the other night, he said to Alice. Looks great on her—fits her perfectly.

That's when Alice blew her lid. Not only had I not returned it, but I had worn it again? I honestly don't know what I was thinking. Alice has names for her outfits, like Catherine O'Hara's character Moira Rose has names for her wigs. Alice once titled an outfit, made of see-through spandex lace, *Pink Heat*.

I like thinking back to my Pink Heat days, she once told me. Every time I wore her, she got me into trouble.

I was sure the white pantsuit had a name and that I was in trouble. To make matters worse, there was a small tear in the back of the white pantsuit. But Alice didn't know this—not yet anyway. I told her I had taken it to the cleaners, just to give it back to her ready to wear. But actually I had taken it to my friend The Weaver's house to see if she could help me mend it. I had it hanging on the hook, in the back seat of a rental car, when I came to pick The Weaver up. She came out to the car and handed me her overnight duffle as I handed her the white pantsuit in a long dress bag.

I'll just pop this inside and be right back, she said. Don't worry, we'll fix it.

I put her duffle in the trunk and started the car. We were going to see The Window Washer.

⟁

Alice is swimming around, investigating the depth and looking for anything rocky.

ALICE: The water is really deep! You can go for it!

I have always preferred jumping to wading in. But I am suddenly afraid of heights. My feet are glued to the rock point, and I can't make myself move.

⟁

The summer I borrowed the white pantsuit was the summer The Weaver and I found The Window Washer, a teenager who grew up and disappeared. The Weaver and I first mentored her, through a performance project we led together in Montréal. When she had graduated from high school, we invited her to Toronto for a few months to work on a new show with us. She was just old enough to live alone, but we felt responsible for her, so we asked her to do things like text us when she got home to the sublet we had found her in my neighbourhood. She took our phones and made us each our first Snapchat account, with the profile names *1 of my 2 moms* and *one of my two moms*. When the work and the sublet were up, she stayed with me one last night before catching a train back to Montréal. I said let's rent a movie, so The Window Washer and I walked together down Church Street to one of the only video stores left in town. She said she liked old movies, and told me her favourite was *The Colour Purple*; she said she watched it every New Year's Eve and that it made her want to be an actor. We browsed through the DVD jackets and she settled on *Terms of Endearment*—because it was made around the same time as *The Colour Purple*, and because she liked the title. She fell asleep halfway through, and I covered her in blankets. After she'd gone, I found an envelope beneath the pillow I'd slid under her head the night before. Inside there was a photograph of the two of us, along with a bookmark that read, "Children outgrow everything, except a mother's heart."

After that, The Weaver and I didn't hear from The Window Washer. Weeks turned to months. No one had heard from her. We started asking around. We tried lots of things: scoured the Internet, called her old high school principal, reached out to anyone on Facebook who had liked her last profile picture. Nothing. No trace of her. One of her friends wanted to hire a private investigator but didn't have enough money.

A full year after The Window Washer had left my apartment, I was walking down Church Street and noticed that the video store had closed—an unrelated finality that prompted me to call the police. There were lots of reasons to be worried. The police confirmed that there had been no record of death, but said I couldn't file a missing-persons report because I wasn't family. I wondered the obvious things: What if she was in trouble and no one was looking for her? What happened to people who didn't have family able to file a report? The officer on the phone asked if she could take down the last known address and send someone to go look into it, but I pretended I didn't know where she had lived. I was suddenly feeling hot and nauseous, worried that I could make things worse by sending the police to her neighbourhood. It didn't seem like a safe thing to do. I wished I hadn't called the police at all. The Weaver and I had run out of ideas to find our girl.

Finally, another six months later, someone messaged me to say they had seen The Window Washer back around her old place. The Weaver and I decided to drive to the Montréal suburb where The Window Washer had lived. We stood at her door and knocked, and knocked, and knocked. The light was on upstairs, so we called out her name. I threw a plastic bottle of Advil at the window that I had in my bag—stones seemed too cliché. Nothing.

The next morning, there were no fresh footprints in the snow. We parked in the visitors' lot of the housing complex and watched all the boys come out to shovel, the girls dragging home weekend shopping bags, and snowballs flying between units from the hands of younger kids. We just sat in the car, waiting and watching the door to The Window Washer's unit. The Weaver and I were worried she hadn't gone out in months. Or worse. There was very little to say and even less to do.

Then I started bleeding. The Weaver said she'd stay and keep watch while I looked for a drugstore. The Window Washer loved Pharmaprix, so I went in there instead of the pharmacy in the competing superstore, at the edge of the neighbourhood. On the way to the feminine hygiene aisle, I saw The Window Washer in the hair-care section. I followed her slowly, past the makeup and the chips, trying not to scare her off. And then I lost her again. Because, of course, it wasn't really her. I just couldn't help thinking she had walked those aisles before. That there were traces of her there, like there were under the snow, where no tracks led up to her door. Like the traces of my feet on that bridge in Kyoto. The Weaver and I drove home, a pair of defeated surrogates. Winter ended and spring came and went. All the while, we wrote The Window Washer letters, not knowing if she was getting them.

In early summer, I decided to try one more time. I took a train to Montréal and hand-delivered one more note to the door:

We love you, Window Washer. This is my phone number. Please call.

There were a few hours before my train home, so I wandered around in Parc Lafontaine. I was sitting watching some kids feed ducks when my phone rang.

Are you still here? The Window Washer asked.

I couldn't believe it.

I'm calling from a pay phone, she said. Can I come meet you?

We sat in the park and hugged each other, as she told me about the unopened stack of our letters under her bed, calling her to come back out into the world.

I just wasn't ready, she said. But I'm ready now. I'm sorry. Thank you for not giving up on me.

I really had no idea if we were doing the right thing, I told The Weaver over the phone as I boarded the train. I think she's going to be okay, I said.

I heard The Weaver exhale, in time with my own relief.

The next time I was in Montréal, I visited The Window Washer. She had a new job washing windows at the tops of skyscrapers. She said she really appreciated the view.

Alice has been in swimming for over five minutes, and I am still peering down from the rock. I need to let go.

ALICE: Whaddayadoing, mate!? We did it! We're here! There's nothing to worry about! Get in this water!

I can't remember what worry-free feels like. Still, I dive in.

I did this call with a stranger recently—theatre on the telephone. I was paired with another audience member, and we were guided through questions to ask each other. My performance partner was older, in her sixties or seventies, not religious, had cats and no kids. Loved books. I think she was a teacher. These are some of the things I gleaned about her, from her answers to the questions. She seemed really self-critical: she didn't think she had courage, didn't dance because she's "not good at it," said she wasn't good in an emergency. I told myself a story about her. But then she spoke so easily of a person she loved, and when I asked if she had ever scaled a fence or dived from great height, she didn't hesitate.

Of course, she said.

I felt relieved. I couldn't actually make any assumptions about her life. The stories we tell can be misleading.

I once mistook loving a story for loving a person. I broke a heart this way and felt very ashamed and sorry. So perhaps I should feel no shame in stating: I met The Turtle online. No meet-cute origin story.

He looks nice, said The Gilmore Girl, as she swiped right. He's a tech journalist—You could use some tech support.

The Gilmore Girl was doing all the swiping.

Plus, you should date him 'cause I need a brown dad—both for the role model and so people might actually believe you and me are related. Obviously.

The Gilmore Girl is my chosen family. She used to live with me sometimes. You could say it was nice of me to make a space for her, but I actually think it was nicer for me. I loved the notes she'd leave around the apartment.

By the closet:

I had to steal your jean jacket—it was an emergency.

On the fridge:

I made some pasta in the kitchen for myself. I would have left you some but I finished the sauce and it seemed weird to just leave plain pasta.

On the window:

Thank you for existing. (I'll come back to help you put up the new blinds.)

By the record player:

There are always good jams to help with the overwhelmingness.

On the kitchen table:

Eat the treats. Do your physio. Drink water. Sleep.

Just inside the front door:

Thank you for letting me think of this place as home.

At the end of our first date, The Turtle was getting up to leave, and then sat back down.

Hey, he said. I want to be completely upfront: I have a daughter, and I live with her mother. It's totally platonic now, and she has a new partner—but we still share a house to co-parent.

I swallowed hard and thought, *Well, I guess we're doing this*, and heard myself say: Okay. Well. I was married. I'm technically still married, if that matters to you... And I'm nearing forty and want to have a baby—so if you don't want to do that again, we probably shouldn't do this.

It was the first time I had said any of those words to anyone. We stood up, shook hands, and said goodnight.

Alice and I are in the water with a family of loons. As we swim back along the shore to our campsite, Alice tells me she intentionally let Marigold ruin the *Sounds of Algonquin* record I gave her last Christmas.

ALICE: What was I thinking?! That was actually a beautiful record! Listen to these loons! Why wouldn't I want to be listening to these loons all the time!? What is wrong with me?! Marigold wanted a record to muck around with and I just let the little chicken have that one. I should have told her no.

ME: You gave Marigold a bit of pleasure. That's all that record was for.

I'm trying hard to be me. We climb up on land beside our docked canoe and it's still raining, so Alice gets dressed under the tarp. I go to the tent to get dry clothes—I need a moment alone to pull myself together. I'd really believed that once we were here, I'd feel like myself again.

ALICE: Grab the fun bag while you're at it!

Every year the contents of the "fun bag"—a small, worn dry-seal blue handbag—are a big debate: what will come and what won't make it. Alice likes to bring lots of what she calls "crafties" camping: watercolours, papers, a plethora of different writing implements. Alice is a letter writer and her penmanship is extraordinary. When I hand her the bag, she retrieves a purple-inked pen with which to add to our list of Dos and Don'ts in the small green waterproof notebook. It's a bit of fun where we praise ourselves for small examples of foresight and complain about things we should have thought of. It's a way of being just where we are. I try to focus on contributing to the list that Alice is presently adding to:

> Don't forget nail clippers
> Save up for our own canoe
> We don't need candles or a big knife
> Bring more hats
> Hot sauce is brilliant
> Learn more astronomy

Alice closes the notebook for now and reaches for her box of watercolour papers.

ALICE: Sometimes I like painting from a painting.

She is holding up a vintage card with an image of a wild-flower bouquet that she picked up at an antique shop off the highway, on a road trip somewhere.

Eight months after we met, The Turtle and I drove eight hours to Massachusetts, to see a work called *Hind Sight*, by light and space artist James Turrell. It is an installation for two people at a time to experience. You follow an unlit winding hallway that gets darker and darker as you move away from where you entered. Each person is meant to hold one of the railings on either side of the twisting hall-way until reaching a chair in which to sit, in what appears to be total and complete darkness. The two people sit in the two chairs, facing the same direction, and wait for their eyes to adjust. After ten to fifteen minutes, something that is barely recognizable as light appears in the distance. You leave unsure of what you saw.

In silence, we each placed our outer hand on opposite railings and reached our inner hand toward the middle of the twisting hallway, grasping the other's free hand as we entered the installation. When we got to the chairs, just far enough apart that we had to let go, I kept my arm stretched out, hoping I could reach him. In hindsight, I see that I was afraid.

We left the museum and went back to our motel room to pack our things. Then, without warning, there was something tangible to fear: things fell apart. He was afraid of change. When we got in the car, I ejected the CD from the player and examined my own Sharpie markings: the words *ROAD TRIP* and a huge, filled-in heart. I calmly returned the CD to the case I had made for it, rolled down the window of the driver's side, and threw it like a frisbee as far as I could send it. The Turtle flinched but looked unsurprised. We drove back in eight hours of silence and tears, except for when we approached the US–Canada border. I dried my eyes and took his hand.

The Turtle asked why I was being nice to him, and I said, Because we're crossing the border and I know you're nervous crossing the border.

The border guard asked me about the nature of our relationship, and The Turtle looked at me as if he had no idea what I would say.

The day after we got home, I went to a stretching class at the YMCA. The room was packed. All women over sixty-five, including the instructor. I arrived a few moments after the class had begun and slipped into a reverent energy at the back of the room. There was something soothing about feeling myself there, led by older women. I almost enjoyed the elevator instrumental tracks accompanying us: "Unchained Melody," various Elton John songs, "Don't Cry for Me Argentina"...

The voice of the instructor was so calming, and the class had been so quiet, that it was startling to hear a woman near the front ask, Is this *Phantom of the Opera?*

The instructor said she thought so, and then quickly tried to refocus us.

It's *Cats*, I heard myself call out. Murmurs of agreement from the front of the room followed.

"Memory!" one person exclaimed.

I laughed, which felt good. I thought the instructor was done with all the disruptive banter, but later, when the instrumental for "Unforgettable" played, she slowly narrated: You can just imagine…someone crying their eyes out…at a dive bar…over a lost love…to this song—and reach up on the exhale!

It could have been awkward and embarrassing to be the youngest participant, and so comparatively out of shape, but instead the class had made me feel I was doing something to take care of myself. I felt strong in conviction. I thought of this line I once read somewhere:

This was my chance, and here I was, letting it run through my fingers like so much water.

I remember thinking that it was the "so much" that made the sentence. "Like water" is nice but unremarkable. "Like *so much* water" puts the knife in your heart. After the stretching class, I wondered if I was letting a life with The Turtle run through my fingers like so much water.

Sometimes being a choice maker is enough. I left my bike at the YMCA and travelled in a daze by TTC to Alice's house, and she gave me the advice I came for.

Yesterday was a hard day, man! she said. Today is a different day!

I called The Turtle and asked him to meet me. I think fear makes bad decisions, I told him.

Yes, he said. I'm still afraid. But yes.

We decided to sit in the dark and wait for our eyes to adjust. In time, we moved our chairs closer together.

⌂

I remind myself that hard feelings are not necessarily permanent, as Alice lays the vintage card on a rock and goes back to the shore to collect some more water to paint with. It's still raining in the distance on the lake, but I watch her walk through patches of sun.

ALICE: Don't move! I need to photograph you just like that, just there, in the light. Beauuuuutiful.

She makes her way back up the edge of the site from the water. As she retrieves the camera from the fun bag to take my picture, I think about The Most Photogenic Person I Have Ever Met and the voice mails we left one another last week.

I'd been listening to a regular guest on CBC Radio. It was a person I knew and thought was nice but not very good at his job. I thought about The Most Photogenic Person I Have Ever Met and how qualified, smart, funny, and well-spoken she was—and how she would be a much better choice as a regular on this show. I picked up my phone and searched for "Hot Tits" in the contacts. The Most Photogenic Person I Have Ever Met had put herself in my phone like that; it was her sense of humour. I hadn't called her in three years. It went to voice mail and I said something awkward about how smart and funny she is—and a great writer!

After I hung up, I worried it came out wrong. I thought about sending her a text, but then wondered if that would just make it more weird. The next day I got this voice mail back:

Hello, you. I just listened to your lovely message. What a nice thing to just like—it was just like so sweet. Anyway, I hope you had a really good day today—it was raining all day, wasn't it? Anyway, I'm just in bed reading and I thought I would give you a ring. Uh, so maybe we will find each other on the phone sometime soon. I, uh, I I I I I I—that's it. I haven't left a message in a really long time. This is novel.

As I was listening to the message, I thought about how many voice mails The Most Photogenic Person I Have Ever Met and I used to leave for each other—at least one a day for a whole year. It made me happy and sad to remember that we were once close. It was a closeness that ended quietly and without notice. An unspoken end of something. We had gone on tour to London together, for a show that tore a strip off the both of us, and I think neither of us wanted to be reminded of the experience by the other's presence. The show had quite publicly crashed and burned, along with the ill-advised relationships we had each gotten ourselves into with other members of the company. We left London with bruised egos and battered hearts. Looking back, though, our friendship was the casualty that mattered most.

I am grateful that Alice and I have never worked together.

ME: Can I move now?

Alice has shot a few frames but is still looking down the viewfinder of my Rolleiflex.

ALICE: You look sad. It's still gorgeous, but not what I was going for.

Alice puts the camera down as I tell her about the voice mails, and she tears up at the thought of lost friendship.

ME: I think I'll write some letters.

ALICE: Good idea. I'm going to get to work on this beauty.

Alice dips her paintbrush in water. I seal an envelope addressed to The Weaver and start work on a new poem called "Janet Jackson." All of my song poems are named after the singer of the song that is referenced within. "Janet Jackson" is a tribute to my best friend in Grade 4, and to the first time I put on headphones. I had been given a yellow Walkman for my birthday, with a *Rhythm Nation* cassette tape, and was stunned by what I felt was a concert being performed just for me. Janet was taking me on an escapade...

Alice wants to know what the title of her "Popular Song" will be.

ME: Hmmm. Well. So far I've got the Whitney Houston and...Sinéad O'Connor, Bob Dylan, Billy Joel, Joni Mitchell, Kate Bush, Lorde, Nina Simone, Cole Porter—or maybe Frank Sinatra, I haven't decided yet—Serge Gainsbourg, and the Pogues. And now I'm working on a Janet Jackson.

ALICE: What?! Come on! Okay, mine better be a good one. But actually, I don't know. You know I don't really like musicians. How about an artist like Joyce Wieland?! Or Diane Arbus? Yeah, call my poem "Diane Arbus." Diane, man. Or I'd take Mary Pratt. What a cool chick.

ME: Sorry, Alice, I think it's gotta be about a song.

ALICE: Okay then, what about Josephine Baker?! She sang, didn't she? Though I'd be in it for the nudity aspect. What a fabulous dancer. And didn't she have a pet cheetah?! Confession! I'd definitely cheat on my guy with Josephine Baker!

ME: She was also a pretty major civil rights activist.

I spot the Kathleen Collins book from last night's reading, sitting by the fun bag, and thumb through it.

ME: When Kathleen Collins wrote this story, "Whatever Happened to Interracial Love," sixteen US states still had anti-miscegenation laws. Josephine would not have been allowed to marry Jo Bouillon in America. Having Marigold would have been illegal for you guys—same for me and The Turtle. Illegal kids.

ALICE: Yeah, right. Wild, man.

I don't think she's really listening.

ALICE: We need more Kathleen tonight. That last story was so good, man.

Alice is not political. That's not where she lives. She doesn't want a history lesson, she just wants the stories. This is something that separates us, but I also think we both find it valuable to be close to someone with a different way of engaging with the world. I usually tell Alice what I think, but sometimes about smaller day-to-day things—like the thing with that tall man on the trail—I just don't go there because there's only so much one can hold forth. No big deal relatively speaking, but here's what happened: at the head of the portage trail, there was traffic. A lot of paddlers coming in and out of the park, and people were trying to make way for each other. Alice and I put our canoe to the side of the trail to let others pass, and set our bags down beside it. I was looking for the yoke pad I'd newly acquired, excited about solo portaging the canoe.

Without asking, the tall man, in a large group of bros, threw our boat up over his shoulders and announced: I'm just going to take this for you. I have to go back for my beer anyway.

Before I could respond, he was already disappearing down the path. Alice thought this unexpected "service" was a *bloody brilliant start to the trip* and said so aloud with her gregarious Australian joie de vivre. I was fuming. I wanted to tell the tall man to fuck right off.

I consider raising this with Alice and belatedly making my

case, but polarization of even this most mundane kind feels so easily reached these days, and I don't want to be navigating here. Besides, Alice is not the friend with whom I would take down the patriarchy. That might be a job for The Weaver.

I finish my letter to The Weaver, refine a line of Whitney Houston, then pick a postcard from Alice's box of stationery to send to The Kid.

The Kid is The Turtle's daughter. The summer after I met her, we took her to Montréal. The three of us were tired from a pleasant day of walking the city, but found ourselves at the foot of Mont Royal and decided to hike up. The Kid was changing schools in the fall and said it would be "well worth it" to make it to the top so she could tell her new classmates she had climbed to the TOP of *MOUNT* Royal.

She offered to carry the backpack The Turtle had been wearing all day, saying, Da's been carrying that heavy bag all day, so the climb will be hardest for him.

When we got partway up, the three of us stopped to lie on some grass and read our books. The Turtle fell asleep and The Kid asked me to come with her to "check things out." We left The Turtle a note and set off. I was grateful for the distraction. The Kid's book was set in an underwater universe, and she kept asking me questions to do with botany, marine biology, and basic scientific knowledge I didn't have. With three university degrees, I was suddenly feeling uneducated. The Turtle and The Kid's mother always knew the answers to questions like: Why is there salt in the sea? The Kid wanted facts, not the poetic speculations about truth and beauty that I could offer her.

We climbed the hill past the man-made waterfall, and The Kid announced that she wanted to find a stone from the TOP of Mount Royal to bring home to her mother. Something about the *mountain* in *Mont* Royal had captured The Kid's imagination, and there was something touching about her trusting me as a co-conspirator in finding a treasure for her mother.

On the last day of our trip, I picked a metro stop at random and said: Let's just go there and see what happens. It was a bad choice. The bakery I found nearby was unappetizing and the "park" I had seen on Google Maps was just some sunburnt grass under a highway overpass. By the time we sat down and unwrapped our soggy sandwiches, I was feeling pretty low about leading us all to such a letdown. Why was I trying to impose my spontaneity on The Turtle and The Kid anyway? The Kid bit into her sandwich and reached for the deck of cards I had just taken out of my bag.

Now, *this* is a decadent vacation, she exclaimed. Great sandwiches, a bit of grass, a bit of shade, a game of cards… What else do we need?

My bad feelings melted away. The Turtle leaned in toward me and whispered: If The Kid's happy, we're happy.

After Montréal, I started writing things down for The Kid. I titled the document *Two Hundred Tales For TK On Her Twentieth*. I had the feeling, or the hope, that one day my observations of her growing up, and of how I grew to love her, might be a special thing for us to have a record of. It was a pretty bold move. A leap of faith.

⌂

The Turtle has another daughter. Unlike The Kid, this kid finds my existence difficult—or that's what I used to think. Now I know it's more accurate to say that she is having a difficult time, and I wish I could help hold her. Sometimes I forget that it is not about me. There is nothing I can do to ensure that our relationship will change. It will change, or it will not change, with time. Sometimes I think about her future memories of our early days and wonder if they will be scars. I wish for her that they will not be scars, but rather offer perspective. I wish that for myself too. I do not write about her now, because it would not be right. Even though, in some moments, she is all I can imagine having anything to say about.

Sometimes I am consumed by all the things I cannot write about. I cannot write about the stark differences between growing up with a stepmother and then becoming a step-mother myself. I cannot explain how death draws borders around the living. I cannot describe the details of what happened between me and The Weaver. I can only set the scene:

The Weaver came for dinner. And then she left.

I closed the door behind The Weaver and looked at our two barely eaten plates of bigoli, the vase of pink tulips, and the full glasses of cava on the table. I downed one glass, then the other, and poured the rest of the bottle down the sink. I grasped all the tulips with one hand and folded them into the compost. Sometimes there is a rupture. Suddenly you're broken and you don't know what you're right or wrong about, or even who you are. I dumped the plates of bigoli into the pot of sauce I had spent the afternoon cooking, put the lid on, and went to bed early with no supper. It was all a little dramatic, but that's how it felt. I wondered if I was reckoning with the experience of conditional love. I wondered if any friendship was at risk in the right set of circumstances. The next morning, I called Alice.

Hey, I said. I just want to make sure you know how much I value you.

Hey! Alice said. You're my...my valuable! You're my most valuable!

Around noon The Gilmore Girl came over and was rooting around in my fridge for something to eat. She saw the pot on the stove and, as I watched her turn on the element to warm it, I wanted to cry out: Don't touch it! It's poison! But instead we ate the bigoli. It was the first sunny day in weeks, so after we ate we decided to go for a walk. It was that time of year between winter and spring when it's any-body's guess, and there had just been another cold snap, bright and crisp. Before we left, I reached into the basket of gloves and hats by the door and pulled out a pair of fingerless mittens—a gift from The Weaver. I stuffed them back in the basket, but then reached for them again. I held them in my hands and imagined The Weaver knitting, each stitch a small act of love. I put them on and we walked out the door. The Gilmore Girl told me she thought I'd put The

Weaver on a bit of a pedestal. It is a strange and humbling thing to have a person you've guided guide you. I realized that if I was ever going to be ready to repair my friendship with The Weaver, I would have to stop doing that.

⛺

My dad gave me some lily bulbs. He calls them family heirlooms. He's kept them for thirty years, planting the bulbs each spring and digging them up each fall. He got them from a visit to a distant cousin who planted and dug them many years before that. Each year the bulbs grow larger or split in two. You can't predict it, but either way, you can store them inside each winter and wait to see how they come back.

⛺

Alice has finished her paintings and is rooting around for something.

ALICE: I'm going to get into this biography on Diana! — Confession! I snuck an extra book in the fun bag!

I'm always in charge of the packing and trying to limit our weight and volume. Alice loves the royals.

ME: Confession—I stuck an extra book in the gear bag…

ALICE: You little ripper!

Alice digs into Princess Margaret's hypocrisy while I read *This Accident of Being Lost* behind a small hill in a patch of sun. The poems in this book are all fundamentally about decolonization, and also about the human heart and the vulnerability of necessary love. Reading Leanne Betasamosake Simpson makes me feel both the pull of things I know to be true, and the weight of things I can only keep trying to understand. I read a piece called "22.5 Minutes," a story-poem about trying not to think about someone for forty-five minutes. One of the topics the narrator uses to distract herself is why she's so fucking glad she's not Kate Middleton. I'm glad I'm not reading about the royals.

Two men pull up to our site in a canoe. They say they are with the park and ask if they can come on land for a moment to assess site conditions.

ALICE: Sure!

Then she remembers my condition.

ALICE: Hold on, we have some nudity here!

But they don't hear her, having already responded to her go-ahead.

ME: Hold on!

I clumsily pull on my plaid shirt, backwards, as they dock, and back away from where they're approaching. The two men are like all the park workers I have ever seen: a pair of white men, one junior and one senior. Junior looks like a high school summer student, but maybe he's twenty or twenty-one. Senior is always thirty-five to forty, often handsome. Senior flashes a smile with his eyes that says he would be completely unfazed by my nudity and might be nude himself were it not for the mandatory nature of his Parks Canada uniform and practical steel-toed boots. Junior has a gas-run chainsaw he's holding like a surgical nurse, waiting for Senior's instruction. I amuse myself imagining Senior chainsawing in the nude but decide the image is a little obvious.

Some of the usual log-bench seating amenities are missing from this site, so Senior asks if he can disturb us by making a little noise.

I came here for the noise, I say. Saw as long as you like.

Senior chuckles wryly and promises to be efficient. I attempt to keep reading at the other end of the site, as he shows Junior how to make diagonal cuts in a large log.

Senior and Junior get back in their boat and paddle away. Alice accuses me of flirting.

ALICE: I thought you were going to invite him for dinner.

I give Alice a look that says both *What do you mean?* and *Okay, fine, you caught me* at the same time.

ME: Being a park ranger is a dreamy job.

ALICE: I think you'd get pretty restless.

I want to be the kind of person who wouldn't get restless.

ME: No. Why? I wouldn't get restless. It's not like being a snail counter.

ALICE: A what?

ME: In Banff National Park, there are people whose job it is to count snails in the spring. There's this little snail there that doesn't exist anywhere else in the world. It's the most at-risk species in Banff—its name is Physella. They found it in the twenties but didn't start counting them till the nineties. Now the counters spend most of their time on their knees, searching for these snails. The largest ones are about the size of your pinkie fingernail, but most of them are like half that size. At some point they realized Physella had disappeared from a few of the locations where they had been in the 1920s. Probably because they live in thermal springs, with high visitor traffic. And it's all a big problem because a healthy snail population means a healthy thermal spring ecosystem.

ALICE: Why do you know so much about this snail?

ME: The Kid did a project on it.

ALICE: Far out, man.

ME: Everything is interdependent.

⟁

I like my doctor. I think if he weren't my doctor that we could be friends—or maybe that's what makes him a good doctor: the fact that you feel like he could be your friend if he wasn't your doctor, and at the same time it's clear that, because he is your doctor, it's not an appropriate pursuit. Each visit we talked about how neither of us ever managed to drink any water because we love coffee and alcohol. That sort of thing. Makes you feel less judged when asked how many drinks of alcohol you have in a week and you can't help yourself from undercounting. I usually lie and then confess my lie as he's making notes. People are more inclined to tell the truth when they don't feel judged.

After my doctor reminded me that, from a statistical point of view, my chances of conceiving were rapidly and exponentially declining, he asked me where I was at with it.

The timing is complicated, I said. Is it— Am I— Is it stupid for me *not* to want to freeze my eggs or an embryo or whatever until we're ready to just *try* first? If we might not actually try for another year because it's complicated and we need some time? Is it really any different trying now or trying a year from now?

My doctor smiled the way he always smiles in his comforting *You have no need to feel like you just overshared* way.

Listen, he said, how about we do some blood work and check the basics?

I wasn't ready to know whatever I thought those blood tests might say, and my mouth was opening to form a question that included *Can we just do this later…?* when I heard him say that I needed to do the test on day three of my period.

Well, today is day three, I unintentionally offered.

Okay, he said. Great, so let's get you next door to the lab so they can take some blood. Then at least we'll know about your egg quantity. I'll also refer you to a fertility specialist. And if you do have any interest in IVF, we should get you on a waitlist for government funding. One round is covered by OHIP. You don't have benefits, do you?

I shook my head.

Well, you don't have to do anything now, but it can take some time to see a specialist, and then getting to the top of this list can take even longer, so why don't we just get you started so that when you're ready, or if you want to, you have options.

I wanted to tell him that Alice said she's sure my eggs are good, so I didn't need to take any tests. I pointed to the full glass of water on his desk.

You're making progress with that, eh?

Yeah, he laughed. Let's get you next door.

I get up early to see the sunrise. Alice is still in the tent and I'm bundled up at the tip of our site making coffee on the tiny burner and looking out at the horizon. Last night I read Alice some of what I've written here so far and she seemed uninterested. I feel like sometimes Alice doesn't want to do things if you want her to do them. Like: *I'll care about your book on my own time and terms, thank you very much.* I imagine this dialogue:

74

ALICE: You can't *need* me to care about your book for you to keep writing it!

ME: But it's about us! Of course I need you to care about it!

ALICE: It isn't about us, it's about you! You go pages and pages without even mentioning the camping! You didn't write a single thing about last night!

In my head I lose the argument: I realize I've betrayed us by trying to turn our trip into a writer's retreat. While we're camping, there aren't supposed to be any productive goals to reach. Only ideas, appreciation, and repose.

Alice gets out of the tent and flashes a smile at the sight of the coffee already made. She sits down beside me and I hand her my cup. She drinks what remains.

ALICE: How about I go for a wood forage and then you read me the rest of what you've got so far while we drink a second coffee?! I'm not a bad friend.

She laughs as she says this, and then we're both laughing.

ME: No, you're not.

We finish our second coffee and the rain comes again. We take off our clothes and let ourselves get soaked and cold so the water will feel warmer when we get in the lake. When we jump in, I am thinking of night swimming with The Kid, on a trip by the Pacific Ocean—an extended family vacation. Everyone was asleep and we got swept up in the idea of a secret. It was hot and windy and we ran hard into the biggest waves she had ever seen. We screamed in delight—her for the mischief and the crashing, and me for the feeling of being connected to her.

I am remembering this feeling as Alice and I swim underwater as far as we can go and, when I come up for air, the rain is bouncing off the lake, and in my mind it's now another season: The Kid's a year older and the two of us are at Bloor and Ossington, drenched in a Toronto downpour. We were shivering, soaked, and waiting for the traffic light when she said: Remember night swimming? *This* reminds me of when we did that—except it's so cold!

When the lights change, we'll be back at the ocean, running into the waves, I told her. Just imagine it, okay?

She nodded her decisive signature nod, and when the light turned green we ran all the way home.

Alice announces she's going to do laps, from one arbitrary, untraceable spot in the lake to another. I follow her for five return lengths.

ME: Let's swim to that island!

Alice follows me. The clouds are moving fast and we swim out of the field of rain-made circles, into the sun. We climb out onto the island, free of words and required conversation. It's good.

⌂

I like it when The Kid talks. Sometimes we're walking

somewhere or I'm picking her up from school, or we're playing a game of cards, and I hear myself filling the air with questions. As if her speech is a guarantee that she is okay. That we are okay. I have friends who have kids, I have friends who don't have kids, and I have friends who have adopted kids. I have single-parent friends, friends who have been to donor clinics, and friends who split with their partners before their children were born. What I don't have are any friends who are "step-parents." The only frame of reference I have are my own parents and step-parents. These isolated, deeply personal references make me feel as if I am undergoing an intense form of applied psychotherapy.

The role of stepmother is a pop culture nightmare. Wicked stepmothers, stepmonsters, and horrible dads' girlfriends are common tropes. Etymologically, *stepchild* is a synonym for orphan. None of it's good.

When she was younger, The Kid and I used to go out and play ball, and sometimes she'd be in a mood that would take a while to overcome. She'd toss a basketball half-heartedly in my direction, and sometimes the carelessness of the throw would catch me off guard, and I'd get it in the leg or the face. The image of that scene from *The Sound of Music* would flash before me—the one where the children are long-faced and sad, tossing a ball with Baroness Schraeder before Maria returns. The Baroness isn't good at games, so the ball flies between her hands and hits her in the stomach, taking the wind out of her before she says, *Okay, children, that's enough for today.*

When this scene came to mind, I'd want to cry out: Nooooo! I'm not the Baroness! I swear! I'm Maria! Except, wait, no—not Maria, because you *have* a great mother who loves you, who is not dead and gone like Captain von Trapp's beloved first wife, and you don't in any way need a *new* mother, and I would never try to take the place of anyone in your life, I just want to know you, and to be an adult you can trust—whom you can literally and metaphorically sing and dance with sometimes—and anyway, I'm just saying that if there was a choice to be made between the Baroness and Maria, I'd be Maria—wouldn't I?

Then the moment would pass and The Kid would be laughing, throwing herself on top of me to get the ball, and the sun would be shining and I'd realize I'm a little too sensitive.

It's the long game with The Kid. As she has grown, the easiness between us has rolled in and out like the tide in waters you haven't yet learned the patterns of. Or like climate change, on a shore you thought you knew. I am grateful to have met The Kid before she became a teenager. Before she began shutting her bedroom door. Before she began answering, "I don't know," prior to hearing the question. Teenagers are capable, in the same single sentence, of showing respect and demonstrating disdain for the adults who care for them. No matter where you take them, or how specifically you choose the destination for them, they often say, with a monotone somewhere between indifference and exasperation, *Can we go back now?* When they say, *Can we go back now?* they are acknowledging that you are responsible for them—you are the one who will ensure their safety in, or logistically facilitate, their "getting back" to wherever they want to retreat from you. At the same time, in asking, *Can we go back?* it feels like they are unabashedly saying: *I am bored of your company.* I've wondered if I should celebrate this directness—there are many contexts in which *I* would like to say, *Can we go back now?* But social obligation prevents me.

When I first had these experiences with The Kid, I thought: I have never felt this way! The Boy and The Window Washer and The Gilmore Girl have not equipped me for this! Why did I think I understood teenagers?! I do not understand teenagers! But then I remembered the love and my arrogance of age that made me endlessly frustrated with The Boy's refusal to "apply himself." When I couldn't help convince him to hand in his school work or see one of his many creative projects through, it upset me—but I didn't think he noticed. Then one day he asked me to stop trying to help him. He said it made him feel he was disappointing me. I hadn't meant for him to notice. I thought then, too, that with The Gilmore Girl, there is a more intense version of this: I know she sometimes feels the pressure of me wanting her to be happy. Sometimes performing this for my sake actually pulls her out of the darkness; other times it is just a burden I've unintentionally handed her. Kids notice everything and give no indication. They might see your hunger for connection in retrospect, after you have no more expectations and just openness, or the readiness to let them lead their own lives. These are probably the stories of the fortunate children. The stories with a small amount of sadness and frustrated obligation, but mostly a sense of having been loved.

I am not anyone's mother. Still, I am doing parenting. I often feel I am chasing the waves and trying not to drown. But when I talk at The Kid and she gives me one-word answers, I try to remember that she remembers night swimming.

ALICE: Let's head back for some lunch, yeah?

We slip back into the water. Alice swims directly back to our site and I float awhile, gazing at her and up at the clouds.

ALICE: Hurry up or I'm going to finish these tinned oysters! Beauuuutiful. Did you get me onto these? What do you think—just snacks or do you want to get into the grilled-cheese idea?

I wade out of the water.

ME: I'll get the fire going.

ALICE: Eat some of these guys first.

Alice hands me a bit of bread with an oyster laid on top and I pop it into my mouth. Sharing food is such a healing thing. A necessary thing for remembering your humanity. We've really been without that this year.

ALICE: You get the fire going and I'll get some beverages sorted. It's brilliant to be here with you, mate.

When The Turtle, The Kid, and I first moved in together, into an apartment near Christie Pits and Koreatown, I obsessed over things like taking her to choose paint colours and hanging pictures of The Turtle and The Kid on the wall. I thought it possible that these gestures would prevent wounds like the ones I experienced in my own childhood, moving into my stepmother's house, where life with my dad, before his new wife, felt erased. It was equally possible that The Kid thought I was trying too hard, or that she didn't think anything of it at all. In any case, the tangible successes of the move were marked by boxed macaroni, pillows, and extra blankets. The Kid was showing signs of interest in cooking, but for the moment, they manifested mostly in pouring powdered cheese into buttered macaroni, emptying packets of spicy ramen into boiling water, or mincing Bulk Barn chocolate bars for sundaes. Having the packets of ramen ready and in her reach, for independent initiative, was a good call.

Likewise, the collection of extra pillows and blankets I got from my mum was stored in our little family room chest, ready for her self-serve. That first season in the apartment, she was still sometimes waking up early on the weekends and liked to make herself a crude, cozy tent on the small couch. She'd put her feet up on the chest, surround herself with pillows, and cover her head in a blanket under which she'd watch TV, as she was permitted to do on weekend mornings while The Turtle and I slept in. It was her Saturday morning routine, and I put the blankets there so she could maintain that comfort.

The blankets were also available for sleepovers. The first time she invited a friend to stay over, I heard her say with something like pride: We have everything, you don't need a sleeping bag *or* a pillow.

Our place wasn't yet home in the unquestioning way her mother's had been her whole life—a house that held memories of her father in it too—but it was a place that had everything she needed. A place that belonged to her, to which she belonged.

Alice and I love making treasures from ordinary objects—just as much as precious ones. But while I love these items for the stories I attach to them, she loves them for their own sake. She keeps everything. She has a storage space in the shop for all her collections. My favourite of her anointed collectables is the "Bad Pottery," the criteria for which is that it must be a) handmade, and b) somehow discarded. She finds it at church rummage sales, thrift stores, and on the street in cardboard boxes marked FREE. Bad Pottery is objectively hideous, if there is such a thing, but she finds it beautiful. Once, for the duration of a neighbourhood BIA craft fair, she packed away all the stationery in the shop and set up an exhibition called *Bad Pottery*. Just for the pleasure of it. Alice knows how to make her own pleasure. This is something we have in common. But she does it with more flare.

ME: I'm still waiting for your big song.

ALICE: Yeah, that's not happening.

Every year I try to get Alice to sing. Sometimes, in January or March, she'll call me to say she's been working on a song in the shower that she'll "release" in Algonquin this summer. I get excited, but it never happens. Which is something for me to enjoy making a fuss about.

ALICE: I'm not singing—even for you—but this year, for your birthday, I will make a speech! I will! I will make a toast to taking pleasure in small things! The speech will begin: "I used to be a *leg man*, before I met you."

Alice is averse to public speaking. It's surprising because she is so gregarious.

ALICE: I will make a toast to love of celebration.

She brandishes a stick from the fire for emphasis.

ALICE: And to the giving and receiving of gifts!

This is the central thing Alice and I have in common. We like to celebrate simple pleasures: having a coffee in the shower, finding an unusual egg cup, good weather, a roll of film, any new vocabulary from the mouth of Marigold, successfully making things from scratch... We like gifts. We can't understand this trend of *No gifts, please* that accompanies every adult birthday invitation. I think we both like giving gifts more than we like receiving them, but we like giving them to each other the most because the other person demonstrates real enthusiasm upon receipt. Enthusiasm is actually the most important gift. We like pretending we are up to something and enjoy the idea of mischief as much as any actual mischief. Alice can make mischief out of anything. She calls meeting for a coffee "going for a sneaky." Coffee and a game of gin rummy might as well be a grand heist.

Gin is the game my grandmother taught me, and something about playing with her felt very conspiratorial too. During our games, she would drink black coffee with a piece of toast cut into fingers, like for dipping eggs, and I would dunk the thin slices of bread into her mug. This was how I acquired a taste for coffee, and cards.

◭

My grandmother was formal, with a twinkle in her eye. Her real game was bridge. My grandma would dress up and play with rich ladies of leisure in the afternoons, before going to work the night shift as a surgical nurse—the ladies of leisure knew not. She had a small, elegant mink stole that she wore to bridge, which the other women admired; there was one player in particular who had her eye on it. My grandmother noticed this, and one day she made a deal: If you win, you can have my mink. If I win, I'll take the keys to your car.

That evening, my grandmother drove up in a red-and-white 1958 Ninety-Eight Oldsmobile convertible with fins, walked through the door, and handed the keys to my then seventeen-year-old mother. Without a word, my grandma disappeared to change into her uniform and left again. She got into her pre-existing Chevy and drove across the Windsor–Detroit border to work at the Henry Ford Hospital.

I have passed all these stories on to The Gilmore Girl.

My grandma died when I was The Kid's age, and my adult self has always mourned not knowing her. Sometimes, with Alice, I feel flashes of what an adult friendship with my grandma might have been like (if I wasn't her grand-daughter and if we'd both been born in the early 1900s, I suppose). The Gilmore Girl tells me these are the myths and truths that hold a person.

△

Nine years, one month, and two days after I took The Ex-Husband to Pearson International Airport, marking the end of our ten years together, I filed for divorce. Or rather, I paid $213 for a red stamp on a document that signified the beginning of that process. When I got to the first service window, where they triage you and give you a number, the man behind the counter glared at the separation date on my paperwork.

This was a long time coming, eh? he said, as if making an astute observation.

For the nine years prior to this particular day, getting divorced had just been an item that sometimes appeared on a list, on a scrap piece of paper, lying around on the kitchen counter, or found in a coat pocket:

Parsley
Alice's website
Get divorced
Grant report
Gift for mum
Shoelaces

While I waited for my number to appear on the screen, it

occurred to me that I'd better let The Ex-Husband know I was divorcing him. I typed an email with my thumb:

Cheri,
You're still at the same address, oui?
I am sending you divorce papers…maybe today.
Talk soon?
Sorry this is such a weird email.
Love,

After I hit Send, my phone rang and it was the intake coordinator at the fertility clinic. Despite my blood work indicating that I had the egg volume of a twenty-five-year-old (Alice was right, thank you very much), my doctor had suggested that, because we couldn't measure the *quality* of my eggs—or anyone's eggs, for that matter—I should still do an intake with a fertility doctor.

Just so you have options, he'd kept saying—because of your age.

The intake coordinator asked if I had a male partner, and then asked me for his date of birth. I couldn't remember the year. All I could think was: The Ex-Husband was born in 1977. I told the intake coordinator The Turtle's age and birthday to stall while I did the math to calculate the year.

Don't worry, she said, you'd be surprised how many people can't even remember their partner's birthdays. They're distracted. They have another birth in mind.

I mourned the loss of the child The Ex-Husband and I

would never have. I didn't wish we were still together, but I would have liked to meet that kid.

By the time I got off the call with the intake coordinator, there was already a new email from her, about a session for both partners with our assigned fertility doctor. I forwarded the email to The Turtle with this note:

What a day. Sending you this from divorceland... (reverse shotgun wedding?)

It was raining when I left the court office with my $213 red stamp in hand. I was shrinking myself from the rain, peering down at the road from under my hood, but when I looked up I saw I was biking toward two rainbows.

No way, I thought. One for each of them: these ends and beginnings.

At the first red light I texted Alice:

I just filed for divorce and got an appointment with a fertility doctor.

Then, an email reply came in from The Ex-Husband:

Hello future ex-wife,
How can you do that to me! You're tearing my heart apart. Being married is so cool! I don't want to be single! I am still at the same address but I will move with my girlfriend soon...she doesn't want to be married again, so if you divorce me I'll be single forever. You're so cruel. Gros bisous,

That guy has a one-of-a-kind sense of humour. I felt so grateful for the possibility of love that is alive in memory, without bitterness. A love that makes room for new love.

My phone whistled with a *holy shit!* text from Alice before I put it back in my pocket and biked ahead.

⌂

I decide to keep the fire going until dinner, and slow-roast some potatoes in the coals.

ALICE: The simplicity of a potato! I just love potatoes! How about another round of cards?

⌂

I had needed a third party to serve The Ex-Husband, so Alice mailed the divorce papers to France and accompanied me back to the court office, to sign an affidavit in the presence of a commissioner.

The commissioner was having a bad day. He waltzed into the Family Court Services office monologuing: All you people are constantly taking smoke breaks. I'm going to take a "mental health" break, okay? I'll be back in seven minutes.

Then he disappeared back down the corridor, past the metal detectors, which you have to get through to gain admission to Family Court—a dark reality. When the commissioner finally came back, the receptionist asked him if he'd informed the previous client about the application for fee waivers.

I don't mention it if they don't, the commissioner said. You know who pays for it when they don't pay? The taxpayer. That's me. Hey, I'd love it if the government paid my bills, but I'm not that lucky.

You have a job—you don't need a waiver! I sputtered uncontrollably. I think everyone in the room but the commissioner heard me. I could not believe I had to be polite to this a-hole to get the documents I needed. Alice told me to settle down and not to concern myself.

He's probably a Brad, that guy, she said. Real dickheads, Brads.

After we got the commissioner's signature, and he'd again waltzed out of the room, I asked the receptionist if there was a way to file a complaint. She looked at me knowingly, as Alice stepped away from the confrontation.

Yes, I know that was totally inappropriate, the receptionist said. I'll figure out how to talk to him about it.

I recognized her expression. She looked like a person who spent considerable amounts of time doing emotional labour for Brads.

Next I was told to go to the "documents room" and ask for my file to be sent "up front." There were a few people sitting at a large table going through paperwork and occasionally slotting coins into the photocopiers to make duplicates. There was a Plexiglas wall that stood between me and all the hard-copy family court files, but no one in sight behind there. I felt like I was in a page of Robert Munsch's *Jonathan Cleaned Up—Then He Heard a Sound*, where a boy goes to Toronto City Hall to seek out the mayor, but instead finds a Wizard of Oz–type character called "the computer" at the end of a clerical labyrinth.

Alice and I loitered around for a while until someone else came in. The person walked decisively to a tiny shelf in the corner of the room, retrieved a hand-cut slip of paper, took it to the counter, filled in the blanks on it, and slid it through the thin space between the counter and the Plexiglas wall. Magically, someone appeared behind the glass and collected the slip of paper.

Excuse me, I started, but the person ignored me and disappeared. So I followed suit and went to get a slip of paper from the tiny shelf and brought it to the counter. The "defendant" and "plaintiff" rows to fill out were counter-intuitive, as The Ex-Husband and I considered ourselves on the same side about this, but the really perplexing part was the series of possible boxes to check at the bottom of the slip.

This file is for (check one):
    Viewing
    Research
    Counter tray
    Charged out
    Not on shelf

Well, I can't get back there, I said to Alice, so how would I know if it's "Not on shelf"—maybe this box-checking section is for office use?

That's when one of the people sitting at the table looked up from her forms and said dryly, You have to check *Counter tray*.

How on earth would I know that?! I exploded, while checking *Counter tray* on the slip of paper.

This is ridiculous! Alice exclaimed. Okay, now just slide it under the glass there like the last guy did, mate—so we can get out of here.

Okay, now we have to take a number in that other room— and hope my file gets pulled by this buddy pretending he can't hear me.

You would have liked him, I said to Alice about The Ex-Husband while we waited. I can only imagine what the two of you together would have been like—a lot of nude foraging, I'd bet.

That sounds amazing! What are you doing divorcing this guy?! I'm kidding, I'm kidding. Meant to be, meant to be. And if you stayed with him, I might never have met you, mate! But what's the story actually? Why was it good but no good?

There was no one in the world I would have rather lived with on a desert island. But I don't live on a desert island.

Far out, man.

Yeah, it took me a few years to come up with that one.

When my number was finally called, it was almost too efficient. The clerk took my forms, my marriage certificate, and Alice's signed affidavit, and said it would be another $485—for what, I'm not sure.

Okay, you should get something in the mail in six-to-eight weeks and then you'll be divorced, she said, as I punched in my code to pay.

Can I get that back now? I asked, pointing to the original copy of my marriage certificate, printed in Inuktitut syllabics.

You got rid of the man, what do you need with the certificate?

I'd like it for the souvenir.

⌂

ME: I hate to do this to you, but…

ALICE: Oh, come on! No way!

I lay my last card face down and raise my empty hands.

ME: Count 'em up.

ALICE: What's this with you always winning all of a sudden?

ME: It had to happen eventually.

ALICE: What do you mean? Nothing but trouble from you all day.

ME: Well, The Kid's been cleaning my clock. So maybe this is my comeback.

ALICE: Oh, she has, has she?

The Kid and I have a "life game" score, perpetually tallied on our kitchen window, in water-based Sharpies. You're supposed to play to five hundred, but we're playing to infinity. She's at 12,455 and I'm only at 11,005. I'm not even letting her win. She hums along as I sing my grandma's discard tune, *I don't want it, you can have it, it's no good to me...*

⟁

The Turtle, The Kid, and I went on a trip to Italy. I was to direct a large-scale premiere at Festspiele, an international performance festival, and the trip was for me to audition young performers, and to meet with some Italian choir directors. I'd been travelling so much that past year, we figured that this time we should all go together—take turns working and hanging with The Kid, and with each other.

It was a strange context. Every two years, the festival, run out of Germany, is hosted by a different EU country, and every year a non-EU country is the special guest. This year, the festival was to be hosted by Italy and the special guest was Canada. (This after some controversy about whether or not the UK should qualify as a host or special guest with

Brexit looming, resulting in the British bowing-out of both roles for the time being…) There was strategic priority money to be tapped, by hosting the festival in a remote, three-thousand-year-old historic hilltop town. Every day, teenagers from around central-east Tuscany made their way in their parents' cars or by regional bus—or some of the older, wealthier ones travelled by moped—to reach the old city walls of the town. From there, they climbed thirty minutes up a footpath to the trapezoidal fortress where the workshops were held. Europe was amid another deadly heat wave. It was, to date, the hottest month ever recorded on earth. The young artists were melting and so was The Kid. We had grand plans of keeping her offline (But, guys! European Netflix!) but it was July and she was miserable outdoors in the heat from 9:00 a.m. to 7:00 p.m., which made her reluctant to take much of an interest in anything. More than that, she was articulating her disdain for anything creative.

I just don't like art, she'd say. I don't get it.

What are you? A philistine?

What's that?

Basically a person who is hostile toward arts and culture.

Yeah, I'm a philistine. And proud of it!

She was teasing me. Sort of. I resented that she grew up thinking art and drama were the easy subjects at school, and that being smart and capable was somehow tied to the periodic table. Then I resented myself for resenting it.

Still, I wanted to get on my soapbox about the merits of creativity and art appreciation, at the very least, as a valuable antidote to boredom.

I remember sitting on the grand steps in the town square and noticing some American siblings bickering nearby.

You know what? said the older brother to the younger brother, who was about The Kid's age. You would be infinitely cooler if you'd stop endlessly tossing your water bottle, stop going on TikTok, and stop being sad.

I was ignoring the Italian choir directors' texts to devote my attention to The Kid. I didn't think I was doing a very good job at either work or parenting. I was also feeling guilty about my level of irritation with The Kid's attitude. Birth parents are allowed to be pissed at their kids, but I didn't have that unconditional bond to lean on.

One night, we decided the three of us would walk up to the cathedral by the fortress to hear a choir. I was feeling more at ease with The Kid, for having relaxed into a casual reprimand earlier at dinner, when she asked if we could *go back now.*

Hey, Kid, I'd replied, stop asking to leave the second *you* feel done with *your* meal. *We* are finishing our meal at a leisurely vacation pace, okay?

I didn't! she railed. I've been done forever! She rolled her eyes at me, reached over with her fork, and took another bite of remaining pasta from my plate: we were becoming family. I held that thought for a moment.

When we're done, can I just go back to the apartment while you guys walk up to the church?

No, The Turtle and I answered in unison.

On the steep climb up, The Kid asked how far it was at least fifteen times. But then, when we rounded the corner and the cathedral appeared, I heard her gasp and saw her eyes widen. I held the sound of her inhalation for a moment—*If The Kid was happy, we were happy.*

Inside the cathedral, I rested on a raised stone slab, under a painting of the Madonna, to the side of the pews near the back. I looked up at the details of the ceiling and pressed myself into the cold rock. I leaned back until I was horizontal, looking up at the thirteenth-century labour and listening to a contemporary choir's rendition of Leonard Cohen's "Hallelujah," letting all my senses tune in. (Hey, I know this song! The Kid whispered.) I felt eyes on me and looked to my left, where a nun was shaking her head and wagging a finger at my disrespectful pose. Being scolded by a nun is unpleasant. It made me petulant: *Does God really want us to be uncomfortable?!* I observed Jesus, nailed to the cross over the altar—right. My mum recently told me she left the Catholic Church because she couldn't comprehend a faith so rooted in a parent allowing a child to suffer.

I always thought you left for feminism, I'd said. To which she replied: That too.

I wondered what the late Leonard would have thought of this whole Catholic scene. I think he and JC were generally

96

on the same page. I was mostly embarrassed for having been scolded by a nun in front of The Kid. I got up and walked toward the candles, put my donation in the box, and lit one for my grandmother. I asked her for help with The Kid.

△

After the summer Italy trip, I said no to things. I worked less on days when The Kid was with us and barely went out when I was in town.

We tried to get pregnant. We'd felt ready in Tuscany, but then held off a few months longer, because there was a stretch of time when pregnancy would have tanked the whole Germany/Italy production. It felt like a big deal, and I'd already invested so much. At the same time, it felt wrong to be thirty-nine and delaying pregnancy because of a job. I couldn't figure out the most feminist thing to do, but in the end decided to delay, to get back in the zone where I'd be, at most, six months along and could theoretically fly.

If we have trouble getting pregnant, it won't be because of these few months, okay? The Turtle had said. No blaming yourself later. Around this time, the fertility clinic called to check in. I told them we were going to try on our own, and we'd be in touch if we needed them.

I got offered another gig in Hong Kong, but this time we hoped I wouldn't be able to go. The timing was right—for us and The Kid. We'd wanted her to be comfortable, and didn't want to throw too much change at her at once. But now she was growing up fast, and we wanted some time together, the four of us, while she was still a kid. The fall came and went, and winter set in, with a lot of time nesting but no pregnancy. I held tightly to Alice's conviction that my eggs were good.

⟁

ALICE: Finally! Gin! You got those aces, but I still gave you the whips.

ME: I have a confession.

ALICE: Oh, good.

ME: ...

⟁

Early in the New Year, I went to The Playwright's opening. I walked through the lobby doors into the sea of familiar faces. There had been times when I'd rolled my eyes at the sight of the "usual suspects"—seeing what seemed like the same people at every theatre event. But on this night, I felt nothing but tenderness. Our greetings were genuine—the smiles, embraces, and squeezing of hands. Between all the touring, and then spending time at home, I'd barely seen my community in two years. I felt weepy. There they were, making things and showing up for each other.

This latest from The Playwright was a piece that gave the finger to David Mamet's *Oleanna* (a seminal text on the male side of the "debate" about sexual harassment—or a male paranoid fantasy of being cancelled by a woman who wrongs him with false accusations). The first three quarters of The Playwright's new play read a bit like a kindred spirit of this celebrated predecessor, but then everything changed and The Playwright, with her signature precision, showed us why *Oleanna* is completely fucked. I couldn't characterize watching her play as an enjoyable experience, but I was grateful for it. As the audience drifted out of the theatre, I met eyes with The Weaver on the other side of the house. We held each other's gaze as we weaved through the rows of empty seats, each smiling nervously at the sight of the other approaching, and finally settling on two spots in the back row.

I've missed you, I said, or she said. It didn't matter who said it.

We'd met a few times in earnest since our ill-fated dinner, to try to talk about what happened between us and the project that tied and tore us. We'd tried to reach a resolution. But our conversations always ended in unintended blame and defence born of hurt. We'd decided to take resolution off the table for the foreseeable future and try to move back toward each other without it. But since that decision, we'd both failed to reach out. That night at the theatre, we sat in the back of the empty seating bank for an hour while the opening-night reception sounded outside. I tried to keep emotionally distant to protect myself, but I somehow couldn't manage it. I just wanted my friend back. I hoped that was progress.

Later, in the lobby, I found The Playwright.

Thank you for giving the finger to *Oleanna*, I said.

That's what I tried to do, she replied, smiling in a way that said both "thank you" and "fucking hell, I tried really hard."

Then we talked about our pantsuits and I told her that even if being at the opening night of her fuck you to *Oleanna* made her want to barf in the bathroom, she should keep visible because she looked fucking fantastic.

You should go home and work on your book, she said.

I can't go home and work on my book because I haven't been to an opening in Toronto in a year, and now, in this moment, it's dawning on me that if I don't start going out more again, I'm going to be in serious danger of not being able to write at all. The Kid's not a project it's okay to burn out from; I need to feed myself in the ways I used to feed myself. I need to be out in the world—I need to model being out in the world for her! But most of the time I don't even have the impulse. I just, genuinely, want to be home with The Kid and The Turtle—it all feels too important to miss.

The Playwright, who has written extensively about the Holocaust, looked at me darkly and said, You know, this is an extreme comparison, but in the death marches, there were mothers who fed all their food to their kids. Those mothers died and then their kids died too. The children of the mothers who took a share of the food? They're the ones who lived.

I looked at her. You're right, I said. That *is* an extreme comparison. But also, yes.

ME: I have a confession.

ALICE: Oh, good.

ME: …

FIVE MONTHS BEFORE
CAMPING WITH ALICE
The Present Continuous

I SPEND THE MORNING MAKING A COLLAGE. I CUT OUT mushrooms from an old encyclopedia, get out the camping watercolours, and paint swaths of orange and yellow between the curves of glued bits of paper. Once it all dries, I turn it over and write Alice's address on the right. On the left, just the words *Happy Birthday, Alice*.

I decide it's okay to go out to the closest mailbox. Canada Post is still operating. I step out onto the street and look both ways for pedestrians. I'm anxious. I see a man half a block away: we nod to each other and gesticulate that he'll take the north side and I'll cross to the south. I turn onto Queen Street and spot the mailbox, at the corner outside the abandoned library. I weave away from people toward it, open the red slot, and drop the mushrooms down. I walk home the same way I came. It's a new neighbourhood I haven't yet been able to explore—we only just moved in. I open our front door, take off my shoes and coat, and leave them where they lie. I walk in toward the sink to wash my hands, for as long as it takes to sing "Happy Birthday" twice. I go back to the door, spray the knob, and wipe it clean. I text Alice:

To celebrate your birthday, I went outside to mail you a postcard.

My phone rings and Alice exclaims: That is wonderful!

I put together a log of things:

January 8. I went to The Playwright's opening.

January 15. I was throwing up in the bathroom. The Kid stepped over me to brush her teeth before school. She joked that maybe I had the plague. I told her to hurry up and get out the door.

January 17. I combed through German and Italian emails. We were on version six of the production schedule. The Italians and the Germans weren't great at communicating.

January 18. I got my period and thought: At least all that violent barfing wasn't my particular brand of morning sickness. It hadn't been a logical conclusion anyway. It was a little early, and I also hadn't been feeling right since October.

January 19. I took Marigold and The Fig to a show about a caterpillar.

January 26. My doctor got me into a gastrointestinal clinic—they had a cancellation for early February. He told me I'd be put under, and that anesthetics are bad for pregnancy so we should hold off trying that cycle. I thought about missing February and how I'd be gone for most of April and May... I thought about calling the fertility clinic.

January 29. The festival sent me an email with my flight details. I was to go to Germany on April 2, and Italy from there a week later. We booked a flight for The Turtle to visit me in late April. We figured if we got lucky in March, it would still be nice to see each other.

February 24. I found out I had a parasite. So much street food on my last tour... My doctor told me to skip March trying too. It's ill-advised to get pregnant on hard-core antibiotics.

February 26. The Festspiele Festival program was announced internationally.

February 29. We moved into our new home. I was so happy. I exclaimed things to Alice as she helped me unpack kitchen boxes: Maybe The Kid will do her homework at the kitchen table now that we have one! No more eating on the floor at a coffee table! Maybe she'll have more friends over! We'll have more friends over! More dinner parties! Maybe with a little more space, we won't worry about The Kid hearing us have sex! I told Alice I'd make a photo every day for the next 365 days, to mark our first year here.

March 2. We'd been wildly unpacking. I wanted to have things settled before I went away. The Turtle and I took the night off and went to a concert. We could barely sway to the music, we were so tired. But it felt so good to be out in the world together, and to come home to this place we had chosen.

March 4. I heard from some of the Tuscan kids that schools were closed for the next two weeks. I hadn't been paying attention to international news. All my communications were with Germany, and they hadn't said anything. I news-filter googled "Italy." Over three thousand cases. I think the last time I'd checked, there were only three—which was fewer than there were here at the time. I read that the Italian government was considering the closure of theatres and the suspension of public events.

March 6. The Kid had all her friends over to our new place for a sleepover. It was a little soon after the move, but great to have them running around. We wanted to be the place where everyone hangs out.

March 7. Italians had been asked not to kiss on the cheek. Some flights were cancelled because of low demand. More than 16 million people were in lockdown in Italy, restricting all movements in and out of the red and yellow zones, with a penalty of up to three months in prison for those who violated the lockdown. Meanwhile, bars in Venice were offering free drinks to lure in customers, while theatres across the country were officially closed. The Tuscan kids sent messages on the group chat. They asked if I was still coming. I messaged them back:

> *Right now, as of this moment, we have not received any official changes to the festival or rehearsal schedule we had planned for May. But of course none of us can say what will happen over the coming days and weeks. We will all have to take it day by day! <3*

March 8. The Canadian composer sent me a demo for the choirs. The Italian choir directors had asked for it the week before, but it suddenly felt weird to send it... There was no lockdown in Tuscany, but I could only imagine it felt scary across Italy.

March 9. Nearly 60 million Italians were in lockdown. The whole country. The case count was 9,172. I messaged the Tuscan kids:

I just wanted to send a note to say I'm thinking of you in these strange times. I hope you and your families are healthy and safe, and you're finding new ways of connecting to each other that might be different from everyday life. About our work together, let's think about ways of us continuing to create together, virtually if not in person. Maybe, as you're home from school and finding extra time on your hands, you might want to listen to this latest draft of the song for the choir? Maybe you even want to learn some of it? I like thinking of us all, in different neighbourhoods and countries, singing this song apart but together.

March 10. I finished the antibiotics but missed my fertile window.

March 11. There were so many emails about the workshops and artist exchange schedule in Germany in April. I hadn't heard a word about postponing, but I didn't think it was a good idea to get on a plane to anywhere in Europe that soon. Alice came over. It was a very normal visit. We didn't think anything of it.

March 12. I went with The Kid to watch her school play. We sat together in the crowded auditorium and watched her friends perform their hearts out. At the end, their teacher ran across the stage, elbow-bumping each cast member. We'd just found out that the next day would be the last day of school here, for at least a few weeks. After the show, The Kid cleaned out her locker; she didn't want to discover rotten lunch discards when she came back. The Kid connects a constellation of people through the two homes she lives in, so since the schools were closing for at least three weeks, the idea of a "family circle of isolation" was raised, so The Kid could keep moving freely between her homes without putting anyone at risk.

March 13. We discussed the circle of isolation. We discussed the circle of isolation. We discussed the circle of isolation.

March 14. The Turtle and I agreed to be in a circle of isolation with The Kid's other household, and her maternal grandparents nearby. I'm still not sure about the extent of it. Shouldn't I be able to see my own mother? I also wonder if this is an important moment for The Kid to stay connected with at least one of her friends.

March 15. I went to the store to get some food. I took side streets and found myself outside The Weaver's house. We're practically neighbours now. I texted to see if she wanted to come outside. We sat—me on the curb and she on her porch—and talked for a while. We couldn't touch, but warmth travelled between us. In this uneasy time, our ease returned: for no more reason than effort and patience. Later that evening, I took one of my dad's lily bulbs to The Weaver's and left it on the porch for her garden.

March 16. The 2020 edition of Festspiele Festival was officially cancelled. I realized how ridiculous it was to wait to get pregnant at the right time.

March 17. I wanted to meet Alice and Marigold at the park. The playgrounds were ghost towns. But it wouldn't work to keep apart from Marigold; she wouldn't understand. We downgraded our plans for Alice's birthday. Our latest thought was simultaneous cooking. We tried to come up with a menu that didn't involve potatoes. Suddenly there were no potatoes anywhere. We each got an email from Ontario Parks. Algonquin was closed.

March 18. The Ex-Husband called to wish me "happy anniversary"—our divorce hadn't come through yet. He described the lockdown in France.

March 19. The closest thing to a live performance in Italy was quarantined Italians singing from their balconies. Local authorities in the northern city of Bergamo could no longer process the number of dead residents. Army trucks transported bodies to crematoriums in other cities because their cemeteries were full. The Turtle and I were day drinking and learning how to play new instruments we got from the Parkdale Public Library before it closed. It didn't feel like death could come for us.

March 20. Because of the cancellations and postponements, in Italy, Germany, Hong Kong, and here at home, I wondered if I had lost a year of work, and possibly a year of pay. But this was not a real problem. The Turtle has steady columns and contracts, I have savings, and our landlord is kind. We are okay. Some people are not okay. Some people were never okay. Over four thousand people in Italy had died, including a grandmother of one of the Tuscan kids.

March 21. At this point we were staying inside. Parents were posting from their cars—sharing tips on respite from their kids. For me, The Kid's company was an antidote to boredom and loose ends. I felt purposeless when she wasn't with us.

March 22. I found a box of old photos from the early 2000s. There were prints from a whole roll I shot on the island with Talking Eyes and images from wandering from Paris. I gathered all the horizon lines and collaged a new landscape, spanning cities, countries, and time.

March 23. I texted Alice:

> *To celebrate your birthday, I just went outside to mail you a postcard.*

More days passed.

Alice sends me alternate titles for the book: *I Should Have Brought You Flowers*, *The Portobello And The Puffball*, *And Then She Ran Away With The Outfit...* My favourite so far is *What A Beautiful Mess*.

The Turtle goes out to pick up The Kid from her mother's place. We've shifted to a week at a time now. The Turtle quips that divorce is a privilege in these times: kids get a change of scenery and adults get time to prepare to "home-school"—as well as to accomplish some of whatever they can manage to accomplish—without feeling like bad parents. Our laptop class reality.

I rock back and forth between feeling like I should be making a *new and innovative* response to this moment and believing that pause is what is required. It seems like everyone is *on it*. I read this post:

Maybe just this once we can stop worrying about self-branding and churning out content and being as or more productive than other artists? Can we take a fucking minute to acknowledge this is unlike anything else in our history? Can we take a moment to be human? The gig economy was killing me. And now we're talking ourselves into doing it non-stop, day-round, full-time, online, for free, forEVER.

I call and thank the friend who posted it, before finally quitting Facebook.

The Turtle comes in with The Kid and a stack of mail, all of which he de-envelopes before washing his hands. He leaves the naked contents on the bookcase and says, There might be something important there for you.

We catch up with The Kid, and the rest of the day goes by. The Kid and I are learning to grow herbs from seed in egg cartons, when I remember the stack of mail. The Kid is watching a video that says we should pour the seeds into a bowl of water to see if they're viable, as I unfold a thin, letter-sized sheet of paper. I look at the red stamp and date at the bottom, indicating that I am now officially divorced, and think: The Ex-Husband was an incredible gardener.

In towns near Tokyo, workers are severing the buds of 3,000 rose bushes and levelling fields of 100,000 tulips. They lay all these flowers to waste, to prevent crowds from gathering to enjoy them. Here in Toronto, High Park closes in anticipation of masses congregating to see the cherry blossoms. Retailers across the country are so inundated with people wanting to buy toilet paper and sanitizer, they decide their receiving staff won't handle flowers; they're too busy working 24/7, trying to keep the shelves stocked with these other products. Flower farmers cry over their growing compost piles.

I watch a robin pull a worm from the earth.

I need a break from The Kid.

I want The Kid to come home.

I make a Covid piñata for The Kid to smash.

The Turtle and I are no closer to pregnancy. Between the procreation postponement, the parasite, and the shingles (my immune system was so low I got shingles on a nerve path that included my vulva—my doctor was in awe), I suddenly found myself over forty, having lost three eggs to illness, just after relinquishing four to my career. I wondered if I had subconsciously provoked my own ailments, because I secretly wanted to wait—to ensure one more gig, somehow always worried it would be my last of any significance.

I write Alice a letter:

I have a confession. I think it might be my fault—

I don't send it.

The small sounds of our home become my map of our family's whereabouts and emotional well-being. My ears are tuned to the opening and closing of The Kid's bedroom door. I track The Turtle in beverages: the click of his tea thermos means he's working; the tchkk of a can opening means he's tired, struggling, and will drink half a can of caffeinated soda; after 5:00 p.m., the same sound means he's done for the day and is opening a can of beer. The Kid is at loose ends when a volleyball swishes up and down through the air, narrowly missing the ceiling; I follow the looped sound of her tossing and catching it, to find her.

The fertility clinic is closed. There's nothing I can do.

The Turtle has this thing where he smiles and waves at us. It's very specific. We'll be in the same room doing separate things for ages, and for no reason in particular he'll make a conspiratorial *psst* sound, even though there's no reason to be quiet, then we'll look up at him, and he'll smile his sweet smile and make a tiny wave at each of us. When we smile back, he'll return to what he's doing, content in this clear expression.

The last time I left town for work, The Turtle hugged me, pulled a face, and said I should stay right here with him and never go anywhere. He said it the way he tells The Kid she should never, ever, ever grow up. He had packed me snacks for the journey with a little note tied to a piece of onigiri that said, *Come back to me soon.*

The Turtle enjoys time apart; he says he likes the pleasure of missing me. I know it's true, but I also know it's more than that: sometimes he just appreciates the sensation of being alone. Now there is no being alone. And so much hunger for people at the same time.

The Weaver is sick of seeing her own face on Zoom calls. She pretends her Internet is bad so she can turn her video off and be freed from the daily tyranny of her own expressions.

The Gilmore Girl is in isolation at her girlfriend's. They love each other, but living together wasn't what they had chosen. It's just the safest thing right now. It's a lot of pressure.

My Childhood Friend is pregnant again. A surprise this time. I hug her, with masks on, while no one is watching.

My mother, the self-described "recovering Catholic," is reciting the forgotten prayers of her youth. She is remotely witnessing the death of her sister. She can't go to the States to be with her.

The Boy is working extra shifts, his gloved hands passing boxes of hot pizza to people on the curb.

The Playwright has no idea how theatre can contend with the power of TV.

Talking Eyes is taking long walks by the bay.

The Painter has more time and is painting less.

The Libertine is liking my posts on Instagram.

Alice is sending postcards to every person she has ever met. At least, that's what I saw on her story.

I try to put on my shoes every morning and take them off every evening.

I write Alice a letter:

I miss you.

I don't send it.

We keep trying try to get pregnant.

I have a dream about my doctor:

Well, the biggest concern is of course your—

No! Don't say it again! Stop talking about my age! I get it, you've told me ten times! You're really upsetting me by constantly telling me I'm too old to have a baby. It's not helping. I don't think anxiety is going to help me conceive.

I—

Sorry. I know doctors and patients aren't supposed to talk about feelings. Sorry.

In waking hours, my doctor calls with my test results. I've had a sore throat and, with The Kid going back and forth, I have to be sure. My doctor leaves a voice mail that starts with *Hey*, in which he identifies himself by first name only. Maybe these times have blurred all our boundaries. My results are negative. He calls a second time, to confirm that I got his voice mail.

How are you doing in all this? he asks.

I hear myself say I'm an extrovert, and a theatre maker, and that I'm struggling with isolation and the end of my industry for the foreseeable future. I tell him I'm concerned about the impact of social restrictions on The Kid's mental health.

What are you doing about *your* mental health? he asks.

I want to tell him that I'm trying to make a baby but I don't feel like having sex, and if I do feel like having sex, The Kid is right there, either with us or within earshot—and I remember hearing my dad and stepmother having sex, and it was an experience I would very much *not* like to inflict on The Kid— but we just make it happen, regardless of these obstacles, because *you* keep telling me I can't lose any more time, and the fertility clinic is still closed, so that's not even an option right now, and how it is that all my friends got pregnant without even trying!

I don't say any of this. Instead I tell him I used to have a therapist, but I don't really anymore.

Well, there are OHIP-covered doctors who do therapy. I could get you one of those. But honestly, most of them aren't very good. They're just GPs like me who took an extra course. They don't really know what they're doing.

None of us really knows what we're doing.

I end the call and log on to meet with some of the Italian teens. We've been meeting online, to fill the vacuum of our shared project. We go around the circle of rectangles. One talks about taking her sister outside to scream, to find her freedom.

Festspiele Festival is now rescheduled for summer 2021. I'll believe it when I see it. In addition to the precarity of all international gatherings, there are the particular problems of our show itself. We'd managed to come up with the worst possible staging for this moment: the audience and performers were to be seated right next to one another, as close as possible, with a 150-person choir occupying the seats around the perimeter of the crowd, singing at them. I know we have to start from scratch, but I'm levelled by the idea that, in this moment, a choir is the most dangerous thing. *A choir is the most dangerous thing*— how can that be? Everything in me wants to fight for the choir. I'm trying to figure out what that might mean, to fight for the choir.

I'm wishing we had "bubbled" with a friend for The Kid. She's in a state of inertia. What's most upsetting is hard to parse: I'm genuinely worried about her, but her lack of engagement is also depressing me. This makes me feel guilty. I don't know what to do for either of us.

In the mornings, before I open my eyes, I search around in my mind for the day. I list facts about yesterday to be sure: yes, today is Tuesday.

I miss other people's lives. Most of us have stopped worrying about joggers getting too close or about passing people on the sidewalk. We know now that outside is better. Still, I haven't been out much. Today I go for a long walk, making figure eights around the neighbourhood, trying to get to know the details of these Parkdale intersections. I see an old schoolmate across the street—I know him by his gait and call out his name. Were we friends? Were we once in a school play together? I can't remember really. But fondness is the feeling that makes me cross the street toward him. It's him for sure; his facial expression is unmistakable. He looks at me, or more like looks through me, like he's offering someone else's apology. I wonder if I'm too close and making him uncomfortable. I take another step back and, when I say my own name, he *sees* me. He leans in.

You look different, of course, but exactly the same, I say. And then I remember: he's got prosopagnosia. Face blindness. Prosopon: face. Agnosia: not knowing.

I can't tell if you've changed or not, he says, grinning. But he remembers everything. He recites one of my lines from the school play. Makes a private joke I would never have been able to retrieve. I'm just glad to see his face.

I am grateful for my senses. Sometimes, when I'm worried, I assure myself that I can still taste things. What a perfect symbol of our time: a plague that literally destroys our sense of taste.

The Kid is making toast while FaceTiming a friend. She props the phone up against the kettle and tells her friend to hang on, while she roots around in the fridge for jam.

This bread is asymmetrical, she announces to the kitchen. It has one big bump and one small bump at the top. I spread the peanut butter on the wrong side, so now my slices don't line up. The bread has *chirality*, she tells The Turtle, who's smelled the toast and is now popping a slice in for himself.

Your toast is an enantiomer, he replies.

Like the handedness of spiral galaxies, she says definitively.

So this is where you get it from! her friend calls from the phone, and The Turtle and The Kid both burst out laughing.

Do you have any idea what they're talking about? I say into the phone, still leaning on the kettle.

No clue, says the friend.

You and me both, I say, as The Kid snatches the phone and returns to her conversation. I'm thrilled she is talking to a friend. I'm thrilled to have heard her laughing.

I get a lot of sweet texts from friends, wishing me happy Mother's Day. It's thoughtful, as they have observed The Kid's growing presence in my life, but it is also strange to receive these messages, knowing The Kid will return home from her mother's tonight, and the day will go unmarked between us.

The Gilmore Girl leaves a red tulip and mixed CD playlist at the door, with a card addressed to "One and only GG mom."

I'm getting used to my neighbour, Loud Talker. I've spent most of the spring wanting to tell her off. Every time I go out back, to listen to the birds and feel the air, there she goes with a monologue delivered to her dog or a dialogue with one of her roommates where only her half of the conversation is audible. Often I can hear her from inside too, even with the windows shut. She once went on for an hour about a special wine she had found at the liquor store, that *no one else knows about*. I've thought about buying her a bottle, and leaving it with a note that says:

> *Here, neighbour, enjoy your favourite wine. Also: shut the fuck up.*

One time, The Kid and I heard Loud Talker holding forth about her dating prospects and how she'd have to wait for wives and girlfriends to catch the virus and die off, so that the dating pool would open up. The Kid saw I had reached my limit, and her eyes bulged with a unique combination of disbelief, shared irritation, and an expression that said: *Nooooooo. Please don't tell her off; you'll embarrass me.* Restraining myself was remarkably difficult.

But, because Loud Talker's a loud talker, I've come to know lots about her, and over time I've started to feel something resembling empathy. We caught eyes over the wall today and she asked me how I was doing. I think she really wanted to know.

I look up the latest restrictions for Ontario Parks. Still day use only, but people are saying the summer looks good for backcountry camping. It will involve some negotiation between our households, and probably some access to testing, but maybe I can make it happen.

I call Alice and ask if she wants to play a round of "online" chess. It was something I could offer. Alice loves chess.

I can't today, we're actually out of town, she says.

Where are you? I ask, already knowing Alice is away with a group of friends and family for the weekend. I momentarily bite my tongue.

I was really feeling the warm weather effect! We're gonna hit the beach, she says.

You can't go to the beach! On a weekend?! It'll be like those hordes of people in Trinity Bellwoods. Did you hear about that?

I hear her sharp inhalation and immediately worry I've overstepped. I honestly don't know.

I mean, of course you *can* go to the beach, I backpedal, it's just...

I want to end the conversation. If it keeps going I'll make things more strained between us, and I can't bear it. I can't locate the nucleus of my anger. Is it that I've been finding her attitude cavalier? Or that our divergent applications of "the rules" make me feel disconnected from her? Am I just resentful of her freedom to follow her own instincts? Maybe I'm worried that, because Alice is looser about social distancing, I'll never be able to negotiate our anniversary camping trip this summer, and all that is written here will never happen.

My dad and I have some correspondence about the lilies. It's an easy thing to talk about.

Here are my lilies from two days ago. Now there is a row of six and growing quickly. I never seem to have the light from the sun on all of them at once. More photos soon.

Here's a photo of mine. I love watching them come up. It's so magical!

The Turtle is reading his Sunday paper. "U.S. Covid Deaths Near 100,000: An Incalculable Loss," the *New York Times* reports. The entire front page accompanying this headline consists of six columns, comprised of lines from one thousand people's obituaries.

The Kid takes the paper, and reads some selections aloud:

Loved the ocean and enjoyed swimming
Anywhere he went, he took pictures
Loved to figure out how things worked
Armed the affordable housing movement with data and
   analysis
Great-grandmother with an easy laugh
IT manager with an eye for beautiful and unusual things
Nashville country folksinger who was a favourite of Bob
   Dylan
Sanitation worker living his fullest days
Known as Big Momma to all who loved her
New father
Could make anything grow

This is sad, she says, putting it down.

People don't know how to talk to each other. Every relationship exists inside larger cumulative conflicts of individual choice and collective responsibility. Action and inaction.

The Gilmore Girl spends the day on a group chat with her family, trying to persuade them that South Asians can be complacent about anti-Black racism. I discuss defunding the police with my mum. I make it personal with the example of The Window Washer and how there should have been a safe place for me to call. In the time it has taken me to write these pages so far, at least one hundred people, mostly Black and Indigenous, have been fatally shot by police officers in Canada. Because there is no centralized database that records these deaths at the national level, there are more deaths than are counted.

Lots of people who didn't understand defunding the police a few days ago are now advocating for abolition. There is a tentative hope circulating.

The Turtle asks The Kid how she thinks she has experienced racism. Unlike The Turtle, she sometimes passes—in Toronto anyway—but she does a mental census when she enters a room. She asks us why she's not considered white when she's half white. Even though she knows.

It's The Kid's birthday. Our households have agreed that visits outside are good, but enforcing the rules of social distancing is slippery. The Kid carefully measures out six-foot stretches and marks four spots with Xs in chalk, for tonight's outdoor movie. We've set up a makeshift screen on the garden wall. The Xs take up all the space there is in the backyard.

This evening, she's been walking on the lakeshore with her friends. They wanted to see the sunset. She is old enough now to spend time out in the world without adults. It's important that she does. We've seen her with her friends this past week and she's being responsible. But when she returns with her friends tonight, I watch through the window as they inch closer together, about to share snacks one of the girls has pulled out of her backpack, and pass around sparklers. I don't want to tell them not to. I want The Kid to have something that resembles normalcy for a moment, but feel obligated to do "the right thing." I don't know what the right thing is. I go outside to where they are, with a tray of snacks divided into individual servings.

Hey, Kid, I say, watch your distance.

We are! she says, stepping back.

I sit down on the stoop in front of them. Hey, guys, I say, listen up for a sec, okay?

They return to their chalked X spots, ridged and joyless. I've ruined the moment, but I keep going. I want to impress upon all of them that The Kid is wearing a heavier backpack.

I don't want her to shoulder it alone. I don't want her to have to be the one to tell her friends to keep their distance.

Listen, I say, looking from one friend to the next: I know you're allowed to take public transit, and I know friends are allowed in your house. You each have different rules and limits that your families are comfortable with. But, as you know, The Kid has to be more cautious, so I need you to help her with that, okay?

Yeah, they both nod.

Okay! I say, trying to sound cheery. I'll leave you guys to it. I toss the friends some hand sanitizer and a couple of boxes of matches for the sparklers, and go back inside.

The Turtle and I need to return my mum's car; we've had it for over a week. She lives at the other end of the city, and we decide we'll walk all the way home. It should take about two and a half hours. I'm happy to have the time with The Turtle. All we have is time together, but being out of our neighbourhood is different. And we're both feeling good today.

We walk along the Danforth, past the closed Only Café, where we used to spend long afternoons before we lived together.

I wish we could stop in for a pint, he says.

That would be so dreamy! But maybe I shouldn't be drinking anyway? Let's find a drugstore.

I'm three days late—I've been experimenting with taking and not taking early pregnancy tests these past few months. Last month I really just wanted to know, so I took one a few days before I was due; this month I decided to wait. I'm not actually superstitious, but I can't help coming up with little charms for the process. Psychologists call it bargaining. It's still early now, but I have a feeling.

The Turtle puts his mask on, to go in the drugstore. Do we want anything else? he asks.

Nope, I say, and give him a little grin. I'm really never late.

It's not even July yet, but it's a scorcher. We are grateful for the breeze and for each other. I have never before held hands with someone so constantly. It's remarkable.

As we cross the Bloor Viaduct, I feel something I haven't felt before. I'm suddenly bleeding, a lot. Anxiety travels through me, upwards into my throat. Finding a public washroom feels stressful, so we make our way down to the Don River Trail to look for a secluded place where I can investigate my body. The Turtle keeps watch while I raise my sundress and feel upwards. A large, unfamiliar clot descends.

I think maybe I'm having a very early miscarriage, I say.

Oh, sweetheart.

What have we got in there? I ask, referring to our pack.

I brought a sarong in case we wanted to lie on something, he says, reaching around in the bag for it.

I can work with that.

I walk away from The Turtle, toward the river. I wade in and let the water wash away the blood with our loss. I pull off my wet clothes, and The Turtle hands me the large swath of fabric, along with a pad I'd stored in the daypack the last time The Kid had an emergency. I fashion the sarong into a new dress, while The Turtle wrings out the one I was wearing. I take his hand and we walk back up to the bridge, to make our way home.

I spend the morning in the garden, trying to revive it. I call over the shared wall to Loud Talker and ask if she has a hose back there.

Yeah, we do, she says. Do you need to use it?

Yes, please, that would be amazing, I say. Thank you so much.

She goes to retrieve the hose and passes it over the wall, asking me if I have enough lead.

Yes, that's great, I say. I only have this watering can. No matter how many times I go inside to fill it up, it's never enough. It's been so hot lately, and everything is wilting away.

By the way, she calls, it's my fortieth next Saturday, so we might be a little loud out here.

(Ha.)

When I finish soaking the contents of my very first garden— the life that has sustained me through this spring—I toss the hose back over the wall.

You done now? she asks.

Yes, thanks again. You have no idea what a gift that was. If my garden died right now, I think I'd lose my shit.

I am missing Marigold growing up. I've hardly spoken with Alice in weeks. It's hard to live differently.

I see on Instagram that she has a new friend. Another mother with a kid about Marigold's age. They're in the park together every day.

The clinic has reopened, and my name has come up for a government-funded IVF cycle.

When we have a baby, it won't matter how we made them, says The Turtle. We're both getting older…what do you think?

When you get to the top of the funded IVF wait list, you either have to be ready to go or ready to go to the back of the line. Because the wait can be two years long, because I'm forty-one, and because you have to be under forty-three to be eligible, it's now or never—unless we want to pass on the $12,000 subsidy and find every penny ourselves. We have a few days to decide. I text Alice, who replies:

Go zone, mate! Just make it happen!

The next steps are watching a series of mandatory videos and booking a required counselling session. I'm very open to the counselling. It makes sense to talk through the process, to make sure we know what to expect. But the counsellor starts with quick questions about our childhoods and if we have ever experienced anything traumatic. It feels like she's testing us. If we disclose some darkness, what happens? No IVF for us? She asks us how many cycles of IVF we intend to pursue. I say I couldn't possibly know the answer to that before we've even begun. She says the only obstacle to having a child is a lack of *openness*—an obsession with biological parenthood. I think: Listen, lady, I already have a kid who wasn't made from my body; you don't have to explain this to me.

But I don't actually think The Kid counts for her. She seems to be saying: You can have *your own baby* if you stop fixating on *your own* egg and sperm.

Forget adoption, she says, you'll never get *a baby*. But there are donor eggs and donor sperm and there's also surrogacy; where there's a will there's a way.

If you have money, I say. I find it outrageous of her to declare all things possible. We're lucky in Ontario to have *one* government funded cycle of IVF, but it only covers a portion of the costs. There is a maximum of one treatment cycle per patient, which includes the transfer of all viable embryos from one egg retrieval—wherever the eggs and sperm come from. The cost of fertility drugs, of purchasing, shipping, or storing sperm and eggs, and of sperm washing, various recommended tests, and storing embryos are not covered by that government funding. And nothing further is subsidized if that first cycle doesn't work. You know what's free? Fucking. It's an incredibly classist position, incredibly emotionally complicated, and I'm becoming more closed to this counsellor by the second. This mandatory counselling session isn't even covered.

Next there's her particular expression of feminism. There's a common refrain in the infertility world, that if women would just *relax*, they'd be able to conceive.

Think of all the women who've been raped and given birth in war zones, she says. Stress didn't prevent their pregnancies, so it's not a woman's job to *relax*.

I'm good with the counsellor taking this *relax* trope apart, but does she have to do it in such a disturbing way? I'm not particularly pleased to have images of rape and war conjured in our conversation about conceiving.

The Zoom call ends, and I'm glad this "counselling" and the scary educational videos are over with. I just want to make it happen. Go zone.

I write my dad about the state of the lilies:

> *Tell me more about the lilies. What happens now? All my blooms have come and gone. BUT there is one bulb that never blossomed. Do you think it still will?*

He responds right away. He wants to be connected.

> *You can cut off the flower stems after they start wilting and enjoy the leaves till the first light frost, when you'll need to dig up the bulbs. Store the bulbs in a cool dark place over winter. It's not likely that your remaining plant will flower this year, but it may bloom again next year.*

The Weaver and I talk about our gardens. We have been working on listening together. Listening and offering. We are working on taking turns. We are working on noticing the other person's offers when they are not the kind of offers we ourselves would make. The Weaver and I are also working on not letting our work define our friendship. It can be painful to love the people you make things with. The stakes are so high, always in more than one way at a time.

Sometimes time just actually changes things, and you can move on if you want to. What time will do is just difficult to know in advance.

I follow the orange line toward the elevator and press the arrow up to the eighteenth floor. In the elevator hallway, I state my name, sanitize my hands, and have my temperature checked before punching in at the computer, where I enter my personal information and appointments. Then I wait to be called. A warm phlebotomy tech takes my blood and a cold sonographer inserts a wand and takes pictures. I do this several times a week, but rarely see the same person twice. It doesn't take very long. It's a very efficient machine. I wait for another nurse to tell me what the ultrasound reports. This is my opportunity to ask questions, and I do. She pulls a vial and syringe from her desk drawer and expertly extracts fluid from a tiny bottle. She returns the liquid and repeats.

Oh, I say. You're really good at that. I feel I am not very good at that.

Our first goal is to get me to release as many eggs as possible in one menstrual cycle, rather than releasing a single egg at ovulation. Nightly, at 10:00 p.m., we collect the following materials:

One Gonal-f Pen, preloaded with medication
One adapter needle
One empty syringe
A one-dose vial of Luveris powder
A one-dose vial of sterile water (with which to mix the Luveris)
One fucking huge needle to extract the water, inject it into the Luveris vial, and bring the solution back into the syringe
One reasonably sized needle to jab into your belly
Two alcohol wipes
A sharps container
A bowl of overpriced ice cream

We place all the items, save the ice cream, on a clean, white, rectangular plate. I prepare the two needles and inject them into my belly. Afterwards, The Turtle kisses me, tells me I'm brave, hands me the ice cream.

I text Alice. The next morning she replies:

GO EGGS!

I sit in the bath, sweating, wondering if I was wrong about it being okay to take baths in the lead-up to my egg retrieval. There are so many bits of information you think you will absolutely remember that slip as easily from certainty as the password for your Apple ID. As I contemplate getting out, I watch a single piece of green metallic confetti rise to the top of the water. Where has this confetti come from? There have been no parties this first year in our home. I raise my arm below the green sparkle, until the lone piece of confetti touches the back of my hand. I slowly lift it out of the water and examine my decorated skin.

I go into the clinic several times a week for various combinations of blood work and ultrasounds. My first impression was that everyone in there looked stressed, unhappy, and middle-aged. I wondered if I looked stressed, unhappy, and middle-aged. I hadn't thought so. No one makes eye contact and no one starts conversations with strangers. Everybody there is going through some version of the same thing, and nobody makes contact with anybody. The only people you can chat with a little are the kind phlebotomy technicians. They move between English and Tagalog, offering words of comfort and expertly drawing blood, in an assembly line of identity verification and cataloguing labelled vials.

The patients at the clinic are diverse in every way but age. Culture, size, shape and style. Most of us are on our phones. Some of us read. Some of us are lost in thought or trying not to think about anything. None of us speak. As if not speaking will allow us to remain observers rather than participants. As if we aren't like the rest of *these* women who *need* fertility assistance… So there is no conversation or sharing of experiences in the waiting room. Still—because of the perpetual Covid screening at entry, the pharmacists filling prescriptions, the women at the desks signing people in when the computer doesn't work, and the various departments calling out names to the waiting rooms—it is never quiet in the clinic. There is, however, one spot in the matrix of waiting areas and doors, out of which people are coming and going, where it feels more like the soundscape of an old school library. It's a small area in a corridor, with four socially distanced cushions on a bench and four stools facing them, staggered, against the opposing wall. It's where you wait to see one of the nurses. Most days I visit the clinic, I spend five to fifteen minutes waiting in this secluded area. Today, I round the corner of the corridor and see that one of the seats is taken by The Sound Designer, a colleague in Toronto theatre. It's disarming to recognize someone here. We don't know each other well, but we've almost worked together a few times. I got her a job with the Italians before everything went to shit. I like her.

Hi! I say, forgetting to be cool about it.

She looks up at me, and we laugh through our masks, acknowledging that we now share a secret. We chat clumsily about work, and I slide down against the wall beside her, because the only chair left is two women away. I'm hoping the woman next to us will offer to switch seats, but she doesn't. She's too busy being perturbed that we're speaking, breaking the clinic's unwritten rule. The Sound Designer and I are now *participants*. We slip around the corner to the waiting area in Naturopathy, which is currently vacant. We'll be able to hear the nurses call us from there. With a little room of our own, our conversation shifts from work to why we are there—and how we are doing in this, and in these times. When my name is called, I tell The Sound Designer to reach out any time if she wants to talk.

Let's go for a walk next week, she calls out after me, as I leave for the nurses' station.

In the world of the pandemic, egg retrieval and embryo implantation are the only two times a partner or other support person is allowed to accompany you into the clinic. This means, incidentally, that there is less waiting-room privacy for men in the clinic than for women. Women can be in there, at any stage of the process, for any reason (blood work, ultrasound, drug pickup, a procedure, or to accompany a partner into a procedure). Men are only there for one of two reasons: to deliver ejaculate in a cup or to accompany a partner into a procedure. For the former, he arrives with the cup tucked under his armpit to keep it warm.

The Turtle and I walk through the door to the operating surgery. We're guided into a small curtained cubicle where I'm to get into a hospital gown. A nurse gives me an Ativan, then puts in an IV. The Turtle reads to me while we wait. I won't remember what he reads, because the nurse puts Gravol in the drip and I doze off. The Turtle is left in the curtained cubicle as I am led, half-conscious, to a bed in a procedure room. Fentanyl is added to the drip, and I don't remember a thing.

A nurse tells us we have nine eggs. That's good! We head to the clinic's pharmacy to pick up my new prescription and supplies. We're at over $4,000 of drugs now and I'm only just starting progesterone. I open the paper bag and examine its contents. These are different needles. Holy fuck, they're huge. I take a photo and text it to Alice. I stare at my phone as we make our way out of the clinic, but she doesn't text back.

When we get home, there are flowers on the steps by the front door. They seem different from what Alice would usually choose, but they're absolutely beautiful. Deep burgundy and pink ranunculus. I've never seen anything like them. I bring them inside and open the card:

Let's go for another walk when you're ready xo—The Sound Designer

I'm touched, and disappointed.

I'm starting a different round of single-shot nightly injections: progesterone oil in the glute. The supplies are only slightly different for this phase:

> One large multi-dose vial of progesterone oil
> One empty syringe
> One WAY HUGER needle to extract the progesterone oil into the syringe
> One incredibly long needle for the intramuscular injection
> Two alcohol wipes
> A microwavable barley bag heating pad
> A sharps container
> The white plate and a bowl of overpriced ice cream

These ones are almost impossible to do yourself—unless you're a slim contortionist with a steady hand.

I text with The Sound Designer:

This is a fucking huge needle!

aaaahhhh send a photo?

I send her the image that Alice never replied to.

lollll 😄😵😭

The progesterone injections are to help prepare my uterus lining so that our embryo has a better chance of attaching. The shots also keep me from menstruating, I think? Or maybe that's what the estrogen pills do. There's been so much information that I don't know what I know some days.

A nurse calls to tell us that seven of our nine eggs have been fertilized. We have seven growing embryos. I text The Sound Designer the news.

7!?! that's incredible 🖤 *(so...no sex for how long after the retrieval?)*

The clinic's communication about when we can and can't have sex has been a bit confusing. The Sound Designer has just started dating again, so this is important information (as if dating weren't difficult enough during a pandemic). She's looking for a donor and a partner, separately.

We used the wrong needle in the progesterone oil, and now there's a piece of the lid floating in the solution. We'll need a replacement vial. I usually go into the clinic between 7:00 and 8:00 a.m., but it's 11:00 a.m. when I'm screened for entry into the clinic's pharmacy. I walk through the waiting room and notice something is different. A different energy is palpable. People are making contact. Some women are chatting across the socially distant aisles. I take a seat and look around. I'm surrounded by a sea of bellies. They must keep our appointments separated so that the ones in the thick of the unknowing don't feel salt in their wounds. I text The Sound Designer:

Holy shit I'm at the clinic and everyone in here is pregnant!

Alice calls and I auto text:

Can I call you later?

We have to sign consent forms for our embryos to be frozen. (Another $800 not covered by the government-funded cycle.) The main question is what we want done with any embryos we don't end up using: donate to another woman or couple, donate for the purposes of research, request that they be destroyed, or pay to keep them frozen and stored indefinitely.

I get a postcard from Alice talking about the weather.

Usually, when you do an ultrasound or get a pap, they keep you covered with a paper sheet the whole time; it's a bit like if you don't *see* them seeing you naked then they're not really seeing you naked. Not for the embryo transfer: here I am with my parts in the air for all to see. I wonder if The Turtle is allowed to be here for emotional or legal reasons—I think it's that his genetics are getting implanted too, so he has a right to witness it.

The doctor on duty tells us we're working with a great embryo today. I don't know how a great embryo is measured, and have some questions about that, but unlike the sweet, fact-driven doctor who did my egg retrieval, this doctor doesn't invite questions. The more he speaks, the less I like him, and I don't want to have bad feelings about the person who is potentially inserting our child into my womb, so I decide to save my questions for a nurse after the procedure.

I have good news and bad news, he tells us. The good news is we're working with a great embryo today. The bad news is that two of your seven embryos died over the weekend.

Died? The Turtle and I look at each other, both trying to understand the doctor's choice of words. It feels like he's asking us to mourn these tiny possibilities, here and now in the operating room.

He tells us that embryo #3 is AA grade. I don't really know what that means, but it sounds good. It also makes me think of a steak house, which feels a little less good.

We'll implant #3 today, and then we'll grow the remaining

four further overnight, he says. They won't all make it till morning, so be prepared for that. Okay, let's get started.

The sonographer turns the monitor toward us, so The Turtle can watch the whole procedure. I can only see some of it, from my position lying down. They insert a catheter that travels through my uterus on the monitor. The doctor points on the screen to where the embryo will be "dropped off" to attach to my uterine lining of its own volition over the coming days. It's so strange that the process, so governed by minute precision, concludes with an action much like letting go of a balloon and seeing where it floats.

The operating surgery is adjacent to a lab where the embryos are stored. The rooms are joined by a glass wall with a window through which to pass genetic material. As our embryo is passed to the doctor, someone announces that they're "handing over" The Turtle and me. The doctor narrates that he is inserting the embryo and, as he does so, pronounces each of our names, saying he is inserting *us*. We watch on the monitor as our embryo travels through the tiny tube and bursts out into my uterus. It's like watching a shooting star.

Afterwards, we're taken back to one of the curtained cubicles. We need to wait ten minutes before I can pee, an instruction that seems to suggest I could pee the embryo out—which is more than a little disturbing. They bring us an ultrasound picture of the embryo implanted—either a precious first keepsake or an image we'll want vanished. While we wait for the minutes to pass, The Turtle and I look at the image and talk about the language used around our embryos. We try to reconcile the fact that we seem to be thinking of these little mergers of the two of us in a Petri dish as alive, with our complete opposition to the "life starts at conception" rhetoric. It's getting scary: Texas is trying to pass some unthinkable anti-abortion laws, where women not a whole lot further along than I might be in this moment will lose their reproductive rights. The question "When does life begin?" is such a twisted strategic mindfuck.

As I get dressed in our tiny curtained-off area, we hear the doctor holding forth with the nurses.

If you really want to laugh, watch Bill Murray in *Groundhog Day*—it's not even dated!

Yes it is, I say to The Turtle. It's totally dated. You just have to understand sexism. Bill Murray is still funny, but it's definitely dated.

It has that woman in it, Amanda or Andrea something, says the doctor from beyond the curtain.

Andie McDowell! I call, but he doesn't hear me.

He's terrible, The Turtle whispers. But you know what? When you were lying there, during the transfer, with the technician pushing on your very full bladder, and you made a joke—I really loved you in that moment.

The Sound Designer and I are strolling. She's had her egg retrieval and frozen four eggs. She still doesn't have any sperm and hasn't decided about a donor. She doesn't *know* she wants to be a mother. She doesn't know she *doesn't* want to be a mother either. She knows she wants to give her eggs a chance.

I've worked hard at becoming the person I am, she says. I'd like to carry on in this world somehow. But I'm considering giving my eggs to someone else—that could be my contribution.

I don't know what to say. I'm in awe of her. It's not the same for any of us.

Before and after the egg retrieval, you have to be gentle because your ovaries are unnaturally enlarged and could get twisted—something like that. It becomes a strange dance of delicacy. You walk around feeling fragile, not knowing if you're actually fragile. The same thing is true during the TWW—the Two-Week Wait. No one I know who got pregnant by having intercourse ever walked around like a delicate flower during the first two weeks of pregnancy (it's unusual to even know you're pregnant at that stage), but this is the hell of fertility intervention—psychologically, absolutely anything can be blamed for it *not working*. In the elevator, on the way out of the clinic after the transfer, I told The Turtle I was still unclear about biking: one nurse told me it was fine and another one told me I shouldn't.

Yeah, I had that question too, said a woman in the elevator.

I looked at her. And…?

Yeah, I'm just not riding my bicycle, she said.

So when I go for walks with The Sound Designer, she's like Bette Midler to my Barbara Hershey in the terminally ill chapter of *Beaches*. The Sound Designer keeps her pace slow and worries about me going too long without eating. When we're walking in High Park, she takes off her own hat and makes me put it on—to protect me from potential ticks. She does I Ching readings and brings me soups her grandmother says will help. I'm ahead of her in the process; she guards me like her possible future.

The TWW is a strange time. You fluctuate from feeling that you're not pregnant to finding every bodily clue that you are. You wonder if you're too high-maintenance and if you're not high-maintenance enough—if you should have been doing more or less. You question your morning coffee and try to define the line between overexertion and not enough physical activity. You think about the hundreds of thousands of women who get pregnant every day who have spent zero minutes thinking about any of this. And then all the women who've done many more rounds of IVF than you have—some with babies, some without.

In the final days of the TWW, I get emails from the clinic checking in:

> *We're thinking about you. We know you've just had your embryo transfer and are waiting for your pregnancy test... We know how stressful this time can be... Everyone processes this time differently...*

They are form letters, but still sweet. The emails offer links to guidance about diet—including foods to eat and foods to avoid—and supplements and lifestyle recommendations from an associated naturopath, for those who are hungry for more information—for more they can *do*. These links make The Turtle angry.

If these are scientifically proven things we are supposed to be doing, then they should have just *told us to do them*. If not, don't send them to us at the eleventh hour and make us question everything we have and haven't been doing to date!

I don't take it that way. Instead I read the emails and think: These emails are written for people who are freaking out. I don't think I'm freaking out. That's good.

My turn to freak out comes after the pregnancy test. When the nurse calls to tell me the news, I know right away from the tone of her voice. We aren't pregnant. I have a million questions I could ask right then and there—Has everything returned to "normal" now? Am I supposed to drink a bottle of wine with soft cheeses, go for a bike ride, and sad-screw? Can I schedule work? Should I keep all the leftover progesterone oil for next time? When is next time? When will I get my period? When will I ovulate again? Should we be having sex right now? Maybe we were supposed to be those people who aren't lucky with IVF and then get pregnant on their own; is that supposed to happen now? Is there any chance the blood test is wrong? Could I actually find out I *am* pregnant—after drinking the wine, eating the cheese and deli meats, and doing a bunch of heavy lifting? But I don't ask any of these questions, because I feel like I'm supposed to be too sad to think of them. So I just thank the nurse and hang up. It's 3:00 p.m. on a Thursday and I figure the follow-up with my fertility doctor might not be until Monday. Maybe I'll get lucky and she'll call tomorrow. I put the phone down and turn to The Turtle, who is still somehow looking hopeful. I shake my head. His face breaks. He really thought it would happen.

I wonder:
Was decaf coffee not okay?
Was the cat too heavy to lift?
Did I pee too soon after the transfer?
Did I strain too much trying to take a shit?

Was it because of that time I rode my bike?
Did I fuck up my injections?
Did I do enough acupuncture?
Did I get enough sleep?
Did I work too hard?
Was I too stressed?
Was I too angry?
Was I too sad?
Did I not harness the power of positive thinking?
Did I tell too many people?
Is it because I said the name out loud?
Am I not meant to be a mother?

Later that evening, I get an email from a clinic secretary, saying I've been scheduled for a follow-up, in two weeks' time. I'm livid. Are you *thinking about me* now? Forget about the TWW, do you *know how stressful this time can be*? I write back to the secretary and ask if there aren't possible next steps to take *before* this scheduled follow-up. I have no idea about the standard timeline after one transfer doesn't work before the next. I write that I am feeling at sea, to which she replies:

> *Your assigned physician is on vacation which is why she is already booked up for the next 2 weeks. I will add you to my cancellation list and reach out to you if something opens up for sooner.*

This is when I lose it. I can't wait two more weeks to find out what's next. Can't one of the other doctors—one of the two who have actually retrieved my eggs and inserted an embryo into my uterus—can't one of them follow up with me? Because of pandemic protocols, I haven't even met my assigned physician. In two weeks I'll be well into my next mensural cycle; it doesn't seem right to delay the process by a whole cycle because someone is on vacation. In the correspondence that follows, the secretary moves from "kind regards" to "regards"—*Hello, I will let the doctor know you are anxious to see her. Regards*. It makes me feel like an anxious hysteric. I'm lost. I've put my life on hold for this process, just like they'd asked me to, and now I'm in free fall.

The Kid is losing time with her sibling. Even without administrative delays in the process, each failed embryo implantation pushes a birth back by at least two months. If we'd gotten pregnant right away, The Kid would have had all her high school years living with the baby before going off to university. A few months is so much of her life right now. So much of a baby's life.

I return Alice's last call and Marigold answers the phone. She isn't quite sure who I am. She knows my voice, but not who it belongs to. Alice and I try not to cry.

We are all grieving time.

When we do talk to my assigned fertility doctor, she couldn't be nicer. She answers all our questions, and waits for us to ask more. She doesn't rush us. She doesn't treat us like we're stupid. She asks how we are and wants to know the answer. We can try again in September.

Maybe, in the meantime, I can carry a canoe. Maybe I can go camping with Alice?

We have three embryos left.

Another summer half-gone. Another hottest year on record.

The Turtle, The Kid, and I have escaped to a cabin on a lake. I didn't want to wait to transfer the next embryo, but now I'm grateful for a break from the needles. I'm grateful to be able to go somewhere—to be able to leave the city, where not seeing people is normal and I'm not on call for the clinic's blood draws and internal ultrasounds. I'm grateful for some time with The Kid, and to not have to decide yet if we tell her about all this. She was with her mother all of July and missed most of the process. She's with us now for the month of August, our month off from IVF.

I thought The Kid would be living in the water, but she's doing the thing of clinging to her phone. More than scrolling, or playing mind-numbing games, the addiction is to the device itself. And maybe more to the exertion of will to do something the parents are trying to stop her from doing. She needs a friend, but it's not my call. The Turtle confiscates the phone and The Kid lies in bed, stubbornly staring at the ceiling.

Alice calls while I'm on the line with The Sound Designer, who thinks she's found a donor. I auto text Alice:

Can I call you later?

When I get off with The Sound Designer, The Kid is still lying in bed.

I'm going for a swim! I say, attempting to entice her.

As if reading my mind, The Kid announces that she's being

as intentionally sullen and sour as possible, as a form of protest.

That's too bad, I say. I guess you'll just have to let the feeling pass.

It won't.

I turn to leave and she asks me to close the door behind me.

I scan the room for my sunglasses and spot the headline of the Arts and Leisure section of the *Times*. "Pivoting to Parenthood." It's an article about dancers who are taking this forced hiatus from the stage as an opportunity to get pregnant. One dancer in the article, at the end of her first trimester, complains that she should have got pregnant right away in March!—*What a waste of time!* I'm enraged. Right. You totally should have just *decided* to have that baby earlier. 'Cause you can do that. Manifest, girl.

I head down to the dock. I get into the canoe and steer myself out to the middle of the lake. I hear a group of people singing "Happy Birthday," kilometres away. It sounds like a party. I want to be at a party.

I lie down on the bottom of the canoe, looking up at the clouds and think: *What do I need? What can I do about it?* I don't have any answers, I just know I feel helpless in all things. I want to go camping with Alice.

I remember our first year, how Alice and I got caught in the wind. As hard as we paddled, it blew us back, swept us sideways across the lake. I yelled directions from the stern, calling for wider or deeper strokes, or for her to lean quickly one way or the other. At one point we hugged the shore, got out, and walked the boat through the shallow water to advance it. I paddled with everything in me to get Alice back before dark. She complained the whole time, but when we finally docked at the put-in and stepped barefoot out of the canoe, nearly capsizing again, Alice's eyes were filled with tears from laughing.

I can't believe the trip's over, mate! I need another night!

Looking up at the sky, I remember nine years of trips past. I think of this year's story, incomplete. For all of our love of letters, I see that this is not a friendship of correspondence. We need to be together.

I watch the clouds darken and part for a long time. The lake is perfectly still. I sit up when I hear The Kid call my name. There she is, standing on the dock in her bathing suit, motioning with her hands for me to paddle in. The Kid has bartered with The Turtle:

I told Da I'd learn thirty digits of pi and jump in the lake—*if* you guys give me my phone back, she calls out with a grin.

All right, let's hear it then, I call out, paddling toward her. (I have no knowledge of pi beyond 3.14.)

3.14159265358979323846264338327 9, she recites at top speed. Come on, let's swim! she calls.

Maybe, in this moment, I don't need that much.

As we walk back up the hill from the lake, The Kid tells me about a dream she's been having. She's waaaay back in Grade 6 and she can't move on to middle school. She says she looked it up on a dream website and it means there's something she has no control over. Which is true, she says, because I have no control over Covid.

We go inside and I hand her her phone. You can still make some choices, I tell myself. I find The Turtle in the kitchen, making us all sandwiches.

Hey, I say. We need to responsibly get The Kid some real, unbounded time with a friend. And I'm going to go camping with Alice.

CAMPING WITH ALICE
The Simple Present

I PULL A STICK OF CHARCOAL FROM THE FIREPIT AND sit by the lake with a pad of Alice's paper.

ME: Hey, check this out!

I hold up a drawing, of a tree and its roots, in progress.

ALICE: That is brilliant! Let me have a go.

Alice takes the charcoal and does a quick sketch of a mushroom that we notice has doubled in size overnight, turns over another page, and then turns to me.

ALICE: Now look at me for a minute. Now turn your head a bit to the right. Yeah, just like that.

ME: I have a confession.

ALICE: Oh, good.

ME: I sometimes I think it's my fault that I haven't gotten pregnant.

ALICE: It's not your fault.

ME: Thank you.

△

When Alice and I return to cell service, I get a text from The Gilmore Girl, saying she needs help moving out of her girlfriend's apartment. They're heartbroken but just can't make it work right now.

Yes. Course. When? Alice and I are just on our way home. (I'm going to get poked up the nose with a q-tip tonight or tomorrow, if you want/can wait till after I get the PCR result...)

Sooner is better.

kk. Tonight? Tomorrow?

Tomorrow would be good. 2?

Sure thing.

🖤 *How was camping w Alice?*

Necessary. 🖤 *Call you when I get home?*

The next day, I drive The Gilmore Girl away from her pandemic-time home, masked and silent with the windows open. I reach over from the driver's seat and hold her hand. She's trying not to cry into her mask. I hate seeing her suffer, but I also know this story will have a happy ending: she will not doubt this past love. She will not regret it.

Before I drop her off, we go for an ice cream and a walk in Prospect Cemetery. I think these things will cheer her, and they do, for a time. We discuss after-death options, and she tells me about the Zoroastrian practice of placing the dead on Towers of Silence, to be exposed to the sun and eaten by birds of prey.

I need to do more research, she says. But you know, I feel like it doesn't actually matter what the dead want, because funerals should be about the people who are grieving. The dead are dead.

I get that. And I mostly agree, for me. Like, do what you need to do. But there are people whose wishes I would want to honour, you know? Like my mum—she has very clear ideas, especially about music, which has to be live, human to human, singing. Recordings offend her. I feel like what I would need would actually be to make sure she'd like it: live music and good oratory.

Makes sense.

But for me, I think I'd be okay with whatever made you all feel good—you, The Kid, and The Turtle if he outlives me.

As we weave along Dundas Street, I remember another drive, on a trip The Gilmore Girl and I once made out West. I'd driven us down a coastal road that wound through forest, and four seasons in a day. Spring turned to winter and then to fall; summer came and went as it pleased. We'd sped past tree trunks, each their own universe in diameter, their rings one hope becoming another. We reached a point and pulled over, to get out and look around. We pretended we were rocks and let the wind blow. I imagined her future.

AFTER CAMPING WITH ALICE
The Future Perfect

SEPTEMBER COMES AND GOES. IT'S BEEN AN EASIER regime than the egg retrieval, and fairly easy not to tell The Kid—because adolescents are, appropriately from a developmental point of view, fairly self-absorbed. She doesn't notice that our weekly beer and french fries night (beer for us, fries for her) has suddenly turned into fries and milkshakes for all. She's too busy being back at school, stepping into her lost self. I love watching her joy in returning to people.

But this second embryo doesn't stick, and we have to take another month off before the next transfer—pandemic protocol to space out the number of procedures, and people in the clinic. So in October, we go on a short trip. I send postcards to Alice and The Kid. The Turtle and I hike the Bruce Trail. Georgian Bay looks like an ocean. Things feel possible again.

The Turtle and I will watch two lines appear, three days in a row. After the third test he will say, Really?? Really?! We will finally believe it. I will be happy we conceived on our trip. It will feel like a good story. The Turtle will just be happy we conceived. I'll call the fertility clinic and cancel my third embryo transfer. I'll find a midwife instead.

I won't debate long about telling people. I'll want my people to know, no matter what happens. The Turtle will be more instinctively private, but happy for me to do and say what I like.

Saying I'm pregnant, followed by masked air-hugs at six feet apart, will feel strange and sad. Especially with my mum, who will bring me flowers for a do-over on the whole announcement. Let's make this moment what we want it to be, she'll say. I'll wish I'd have hugged her, feel I followed the wrong risk assessments.

My breasts will feel like melons, I'll have to pee all the time, I'll mostly eat cottage cheese. I will hear the heartbeat.

The day I hear the heartbeat, The Kid will break her arm at school. She'll be so excited to be on a team again, she'll go a little overboard. She'll want to play out the game, but her arm will be Jell-O, so she'll reluctantly call home. I'll tell The Turtle to go get her—my mum will drive me to the seven-week ultrasound. It will make her happy to take me anyway. She won't be allowed to come in with me, so I'll sit in the waiting room window, so she can see me from her car across the street. We'll mime exaggerated expressions and text each other jokes.

I'll come out of the clinic with a picture of a sound wave—
122 beats per minute. My mum will ask if she can keep it.

The Turtle and I will talk about when to tell The Kid. We'll
consider the end of the first trimester, which will fall on
Christmas Day. But Christmas Day will seem like a lot of
pressure. We'll wonder if she'll need time to process. We also
won't feel right about keeping the secret. In considering the
reasons not to tell her sooner, the only thing we'll come up
with is protecting her from a potentially hard thing. What
would that mean? we'll ask. To pretend we weren't going
through something important. To keep sadness a secret.
We'll decide to model strength in the face of uncertainty,
and resilience if it comes to it. We'll want to be a family who
can talk about hard things. It's your baby too, we'll tell her,
so you get to know about it, even though there are risks.
Whatever happens, we'll be okay, we'll say.

We'll decide to tell The Kid at almost ten weeks, when we'll
have her home for the week that follows, so there'll be time
to adjust together, if adjustment is needed. We'll tell her
while we're decorating the tree. When we tell her she'll cry,
hug me, and squeal: Really?? Really?! echoing her father's
reaction. She'll be happy. I'll be so happy she's happy.

We'll begin the competition for names. We'll talk about
having a little one next Christmas. The Kid will buy yellow
yarn and begin knitting a blanket. She'll imagine her life
with a sibling. She'll calculate the future, saying: I'm going
to be so old when the baby is my age! I'll be the cool adult!

At the end of that week together, dreaming, I will wake up
in the night, feeling liquid between my legs. We'll wait until

morning to call the midwife, who'll tell us its fifty-fifty: spotting could be a perfectly normal part of a health pregnancy, or it could be the beginning of a miscarriage. The only way to know will be an ultrasound, so we'll have to wait out the weekend. She won't advise going to emergency, now that case counts are going up again—It won't change the results of our coin toss. Okay. Strength in the face of uncertainty, I'll think. I'll think about the people I've told, and wonder if I've made a mistake.

I'll tell The Kid I'm nauseous and take it easy. The day will come and go without incident. I'll think we're safe. The Kid will go back to her other house, and The Turtle and I will pass the time until we go to bed. I will wake up hemorrhaging and writhe in agony for hours. There will be no question, but I will still doubt it. The Turtle will read to me, from a book we will never read again.

On Monday morning, we'll go for an ultrasound. We'll wait outside for the midwife to send the requisition. She'll accidentally fax the report from my last ultrasound: 122/bpm—the heartbeat The Turtle will never hear. I'll go in alone. The technician will say she can't tell me anything. She'll apologize for this. On my way out, I'll catch a glimpse of the monitor, and see that my uterus is empty.

The midwife will call to confirm. We'll drive to The Kid's other house and ask her to come out. We'll tell her right away; we won't want to build worry. The three of us will cry quietly in the car. She will decide to stay the night with us. We'll all crawl into bed together and fall asleep at five o'clock in the afternoon.

When we wake at eight, there'll be gentleness. My mother will come over, and come inside for the first time in ten months. I'll hug her, tightly, like I'll wish I'd have done with the good news. She'll bring The Kid her Christmas presents early. It will feel nice, not forced. The Kid will keep close. She'll lay her head on my shoulder. She'll pick a present from under the tree, and hand it to my mum. A framed portrait of the three of us—The Kid's idea. When my mother leaves, The Kid will make a joke about grandmas. A new designation. It will be the definition of bittersweet.

We'll eat the dinner my mum has brought for us. The Turtle and I will open the bottle of wine we brought back from Italy. The one with "For a day when we need it," written on the box. We'll watch *The Sound of Music*, a holiday tradition. We'll sing "My Favorite Things." We'll let The Kid sleep in the next morning and go late to school.

The days that follow will be a blur. I'll look around our room at night and disassemble the changes we had planned: we won't have to switch sides of the bed so that it's easier for me to get in and out; we won't need to move out one of our desks to make room for a cradle… But cards and soup will arrive on our porch, and these things will make me feel better. I won't feel alone. I won't feel like I have to avoid my friends. I'll be able to talk to them, or rest easy knowing they'll know why I'm not taking to them. I won't have to hide from The Kid, and I won't fall apart: she'll see I'm not falling apart. She'll say that when we do have a baby, we're going to have a complicated family tree. She'll know we haven't given up. She'll hold the hope with us. She'll tell her best friend about our loss—an uncharacteristic sharing for her. Something will have shifted. It'll all be okay to talk about. We'll tell The Kid that if we get pregnant again, this time we'll call it The Maybe for a full thirteen weeks. An extra week for good measure. We can call it The Baby after that. Alice will bring flowers. As time passes, I'll survey them wilting, salvaging what I can with each reduction of the arrangement. Trimming the ends, I'll hang some to dry, over the days that follow.

I'll be surprised to find I know more women who've had miscarriages than haven't. The Playwright, Talking Eyes, The Most Photogenic Person I Have Ever Met, my grand-mother... I'll have had no idea. I'll see a heaving belly on the street, and for the first time I'll wonder if other possible babies might have been lost before this round promise. I'll think that part of making a baby is often losing a baby. I'll learn, again, that you never know other people's stories.

Alice will book us a spring camping trip. Something to look forward to.

At my third ultrasound for this pregnancy, the one to make sure that everything is all right after everything was not all right, the sonographer will ask how far along I had been. I'll say eleven weeks and she'll say, Darn, shaking her head. I'll find it very sweet. She'll ask if I have other children, and I'll say, Yes, but not from my body. She'll say, Well, that's okay!—that's good too!

Do I want to have a child? This question waits for every person with a womb. But it's a myth that deciding to make a baby means that you will. And when you do mothering without giving birth, it can take a long time to accept your motherhood. Will I ever be a mother? Am I one already? How do I live in the unknowing?

NOW
The Conditional

WE TAKE THE KID ON A NIGHT WALK, THROUGH AN open-air installation.

THE KID: Do I have to go?

ME: Yes.

THE KID: Me? The philistine?!

She grins.

I tell The Turtle that we should stop telling her things are *art*. We could have just said it was a light show made out of heartbeats—we could have told her it was *science*, I say.

The piece is a canopy of light bulbs, hung like an upside-down mountain range. Three sensors hang amongst them, and people take turns offering out their palms, for the bulbs to pulse at the rate of their hearts. Layer upon layer of every visitor's heartbeat is stored in the topological electric repository.

The work was inspired by an ultrasound of the artist's twins. The artist had requested that a second ultrasound machine be brought in, so he and his wife could hear both heart-beats at once. There was something about the differences between those two potential beings already, he said, and something about what was only possible in hearing them together.

I think about our two remaining embryos, in waiting.

I told you we should have twins, The Kid says, her eyebrows raised. Two Maybes are better than one, she says, before racing off to the next sensor.

I write this all down. Another entry for her.

At home in the garden, The Kid and I are hanging a bird feeder. I have an idea! she announces, darting inside.

Loud Talker is on the other side of the garden wall, having a smoke.

Your kid is like, really into hanging out with you, she calls over. I thought teenagers were supposed to hate their parents.

Before I can answer, The Kid returns with a string of lights.

AUTHOR'S NOTE

"Any incident is filtered subjectively, which causes memoirs and oral histories to be compelling as much for their versions of honesty, what they remember, the facts of their lives, as for their untrustworthiness, misinformation, and bias... Whether fiction or nonfiction, any story or account represents the storyteller's."
—Lynne Tillman, *Mothercare*

Any story or account represents the teller's in the moment she is doing the telling. Time rarely leaves perspective unchanged.

While this book recounts real events, describes realized artworks, and draws from my own impressions and experiences of living, it is also a work of fiction that seeks only to be true to itself.

ACKNOWLEDGEMENTS

Tayo, Zaylie, and Jet: You three have been my doorways to so many new understandings of love. Mark Brubacher, Cara Cole, Phillipa Croft, Jane Danielson, Theo Gallero, Ofa Gasesepe, Joan Green, Vivien Jaboeuf, Erum Khan, Evalyn Parry, Eleanore Payne, Zoe Shye, Naomi Skwarna, Cara Spooner, Dennis Sutherland, Jacob Wren, and Helen Yung: Thank you for the heart-holding through so many songs. Richard Lachman, you are my other half of a broken whole.

Hannah Moscovitch, my first editorial sounding board (or book doula), was nice to me when I needed it, but only when she meant it. She also told me to shut up and write. Both of these approaches were very valuable. Erum Khan was my first inner-circle reader. Anna Lee Popham was a critical and crucial outside eye at essential moments. Sherri Hay guided me through the poetry of tenses. My editor, Malcolm Sutton, both listened and provided thoughtful counsel at the end of the writing journey. He also brought the watercolours, for which I am grateful. Jordan Tannahill was a trusted advisor in the lead-up to publication. Hazel and Jay Millar are in some ways responsible for this becoming a book at all. I am grateful.

The piece described in the final pages of this book is an imagined iteration of *Pulse Topology* by Rafael Lozano-Hemmer. The "theatre on the telephone" referenced on page 53 was *A Thousand Ways (Part One): A Phone Call*, by 600 Highwaymen, presented by Canadian Stage in Toronto in 2020. The pregnant writer in the bar on page 26 was Zadie Smith, as recounted in *Slate*. The quote on page 59 is paraphrased from the line "It was my first big chance, but here I was, sitting back and letting it run through my fingers like so much water," from Sylvia Plath's *The Bell Jar*. The photographs on pages 33 and 34 are from my own photographic series, *Readers* (2008).

The writing of this book was supported by the Canada Council for the Arts, the Ontario Arts Council, and the Toronto Arts Council, with funding from the City of Toronto.

ABOUT THE AUTHOR

Erin Brubacher is a multidisciplinary artist. She is the author of the poetry collection *In the small hours: Thirty-nine months & seven days* (Gaspereau Press) and co-author of the hybrid performance-based book *7th Cousins: An Automythography* (Book*hug Press). Her award-winning work in theatre has taken her to contexts including the National Arts Centre (Ottawa), the Aga Khan Museum (Toronto), Festival Internacional Cervantino (Mexico), Theater der Welt (Germany), and the Edinburgh International Festival (UK). She is driven by the desire to make meeting places: for her, art is a framework that serves to gather people who might not otherwise be in a literal or figurative room together. Erin lived in ten cities before returning to Toronto, where she makes a home with her husband and four children.

PHOTO: PHILLIPA CROFT

COLOPHON

Manufactured as the first edition of
These Songs I Know By Heart
in the spring of 2024 by Book*hug Press

Edited for the press by Malcolm Sutton
Copy-edited by Stuart Ross
Proofread by Laurie Siblock
Type + design by Malcolm Sutton
Set in ITC Galliard

Printed in Canada

bookhugpress.ca